# A Note to Rea

While the Farley and Etingoff families
that happened in Cincinnati during 1832 are not. Cincinnati had
one of the worst floods in history and was barely recovering from
that disaster when cholera struck.

Dr. Daniel Drake, who befriends Rob and Emma in this story,
is a historical figure. While his theory about "invisible insects" that
spread disease was eventually proven wrong, he came very close to
discovering germs. His efforts to get people in Cincinnati to clean
up the rotting animal carcasses and other garbage in their streets
after the flood is credited with saving hundreds of lives. While
more than eight hundred people died in Cincinnati during the
cholera epidemic of 1832–33, many more lives would have been
lost without Dr. Drake's cleanup efforts.

SISTERS IN TIME

# Emma's
## Secret

THE CINCINNATI EPIDEMIC

VEDA BOYD JONES

BARBOUR
PUBLISHING

# Emma's
## Secret

*For Morgan*

Cover design by Lookout Design Group, Inc.

Published by Barbour Publishing, Inc., P.O. Box 719, Uhrichsville, Ohio 44683 www.barbourbooks.com

*Our mission is to publish and distribute inspirational products offering exceptional value and biblical encouragement to the masses.*

 Member of the
Evangelical Christian
Publishers Association

Printed in the United States of America.
5 4 3 2 1

# CONTENTS

CHAPTER 1

# The Great Ohio Flood

Emma Farley bit her lip, trying to hold back her worry.

"The river's rising," her cousin, Rob Etingoff, told his father. "The men at the wharf say it's up three feet in the last hour. They're moving wagon loads to higher ground."

Emma and Rob had detoured by the public landing on their way to his father's shipyard, where Rob was the cleanup boy after school. Rob was actually her cousin a few times removed. Their families jokingly called each other distant cousins because Emma's family lived on a farm outside of town and Rob's lived smack inside Cincinnati. They went to the same school, though, and they had been best friends all their lives.

"We'll go under," Rob's father said matter-of-factly. "I've got three men loading the steam engines. Go on to the toolshed and start to help. I'll send someone else out as soon as I can."

"Can I help, Uncle Anthony?" Emma asked. She wanted to do something, too.

Anthony Etingoff gave her a small smile. "We could use as many hands as possible. Just don't get in the way of the men."

Emma nodded and ran after Rob into a small brick building.

The mighty Ohio flooded every spring, but it usually waited until later in the year. Now, even inside the shed, Emma could hear the river's roar. Of course, the shipyard was near the river so that new ships could be launched easily into the water.

"Will it flood?" she asked Rob.

He shrugged. "Sometimes the shipyard goes under water. Sometimes it doesn't."

It had rained for two days, but that wasn't the only thing making the river rise. The rain and melting snow on the western slopes of the Allegheny Mountains fed small streams and the big rivers near Pittsburgh—and eventually they all flowed into the Ohio River. Odd that something so far away could affect them here in Cincinnati.

Rob handed Emma a pair of leather gloves. She pulled them on and helped him fill a wheelbarrow with hammers, wedges, chisels, and saws. The leather gloves protected her hands from the cold metal, but the tools were heavy. Soon her arms and fingers began to ache. Once they filled the cart, Rob pushed it to the main building, with Emma tagging along behind him. She didn't know what else to do, though she wished she could be more help.

Rob's father was busy loading record books onto a flatbed wagon.

"Where should I take the wheelbarrow?" Rob asked him.

While she waited, Emma glanced toward the rising river water, which was nearing the base of the new sign: ETINGOFF SHIPYARD. QUALITY STEAMBOATS. ANTHONY ETINGOFF, OWNER. She knew the last sign had been washed away a year ago. But this time, Uncle Anthony had made a sign he said should withstand the Ohio's fury. The supports were brick, and the sign hung a good twelve feet aboveground.

Instead of answering Rob, Uncle Anthony called to a nearby worker, who helped Rob lift the wheelbarrow onto the wagon. Then Uncle Anthony turned to Rob. "Did you get everything?"

"No. Some chains and ropes are still in the shed. We'll go fill another barrow."

Uncle Anthony nodded, and Emma and Rob ran toward the shed.

"Rob, Emma, wait!"

The children turned around.

"Go check on the Davis sisters. See if they'll come to our house."

Rob and Emma changed directions and ran toward Plum Street. The cold wind that had been blocked by buildings at the shipyard hit Emma full force as they dashed down Front Street. At least the downpour had ended at noon, but the sun had never broken through the thick gray clouds. They looked like snow clouds, which would have been more likely in mid-February than all this rain.

When they came to the cross streets, Emma looked down them toward the river. She could see churning floodwaters now threatening Water Street. It always went under, seemed like, so it had been well named.

Last spring, Emma remembered, the Davis sisters wouldn't leave their home. They insisted the flood wouldn't reach their house, and they'd been right. But Emma thought the look and feel of the water was different this year. Emma pulled her wool coat closer around her neck against the chilly wind. Rob shivered and pulled his cap lower on his head, leaving only a thatch of blond hair sticking out at the back. As he sprinted ahead of her, Emma followed, doing her best to keep up, though her side was aching now from running. As she went, she was bombarded by the sound of men yelling orders, horses neighing as they pulled heavy loads toward higher ground, and women's high-pitched voices as they passed, carrying household items and hustling children away from the river's encroaching waters.

Emma was out of breath by the time they reached Plum Street. She was sweating under her coat, but she could see her breath in the frigid air.

Rob knocked on the door of the two-story brick house and hollered, "Miss Clara!"

A moment later, Miss Clara Davis opened the door. "Hello, children. Come in."

They stepped inside the hall and shut the door quickly behind them so the winter air wouldn't enter the house. "Father sent me to ask you to go to our house," Rob said. "The water's bound to reach your home this year."

"Now, Rob, I've seen a few more floods than you have." Miss Clara laughed. She always laughed after she said something; Emma thought it was an odd habit. "The water won't get this high."

"We're moving the engines and machinery," Rob said in an effort to convince her.

"We're moving some of our belongings upstairs, just in case," she said. "Ruthann insists, but I don't think we're in any danger."

Emma glanced down the hall to the parlor. Although furniture was still in place, lamps and some of Miss Clara's decorative figurines were missing. Miss Ruthann's frail figure appeared at the top of the stairs, and she slowly made her way down, holding on to the railing.

"Are you here to help us take things upstairs?" she asked in her soft, quavering voice. She was the elder of the two sisters, and Emma guessed she must be nearing seventy.

"We could use the help," Miss Clara added. She was at least five years younger than her sister, although she looked younger than that, probably because she got around so much better. She also weighed twice what her sister weighed and had that loud laugh.

Emma and Rob exchanged looks, and Rob rolled his eyes behind Miss Clara's back. "For a few minutes," he said. "Father's expecting us back at the yard." Emma knew he was eager to go back and help his father—but she also knew Uncle Anthony would want him to help the Davis sisters. They ate Sunday dinner with the Etingoffs nearly every week after church, and Emma had often heard Rob's father say he had known the sisters long before Rob and Emma were born.

As quickly as they could, Emma and Rob climbed the stairs, loaded down with foodstuffs and kitchen utensils. They made several trips, carrying chairs and small tables. Then they helped Miss Clara carry the heavy dining room table.

"You'll come back tomorrow and help us carry all this back down, won't you?" Miss Clara asked.

"Yes, ma'am," Rob answered.

"It won't be tomorrow," Miss Ruthann said. "The river's taking control."

Miss Ruthann obviously agreed with Rob's opinion of the flood. "Then why don't you go to our house where you'll be out of the river's reach?" he asked.

"Oh, we couldn't leave Papa's house," Miss Ruthann said. "We'll be fine."

Emma glanced at the mantle clock as she grabbed it and carried it upstairs. Their few minutes of helping had turned into an hour already. She knew her mother would be wondering where she was. But she couldn't leave Rob alone to help these women carry their treasures upstairs.

Miss Ruthann made one trip for every six of Emma's and Rob's. Miss Clara lumbered up and down twice as fast as her sister, but she was still painstakingly slow. Rob looked at Emma and sighed.

"What else do you want carried upstairs?" he asked the sisters.

"What about that trunk of Mama's in the back room?" Miss Ruthann asked.

"Oh, yes, we'll need that upstairs," Miss Clara agreed, and Rob hurried to fetch the trunk. Emma giggled to herself; it was one of the few times she'd heard the two sisters agree on anything.

After another dozen trips up the stairs, Emma heard a commotion outside. Earlier there had been the noise of people hurrying by, carrying boxes or driving teams of horses, but this was different.

"It's surging," she heard someone call.

She and Rob raced to the window and saw muddy river water rushing toward them. Both women were upstairs; Rob took the stairs two at a time.

"It's coming," Emma heard him yell as she followed him upstairs more slowly.

The sisters were already at the bedroom window, looking down on the street below.

"It can't get this high," Miss Clara said. "It might get in the cellar, but this house is built too far off the ground to be in any danger."

Emma bit back her impatience. She didn't want to argue with the old woman, but panic was building inside her. Doing everything in her power not to scream, she looked at Rob, but she knew he was as helpless as she was.

"Dear God, help us be safe," Miss Ruthann prayed. Rob added his "Amen" in a high voice Emma barely recognized.

"Run down and get some firewood," Miss Clara ordered him. "The wood box in the kitchen is full."

Emma knew Rob didn't want to leave the scene at the window,

but he did as he was told. Emma waited with the sisters, too tired and scared to move. On Rob's second trip back from the kitchen, Emma noticed his feet were wet. The third time he came back upstairs, the bottom of his pant legs were dark and damp; the water must have already been creeping into the downstairs room. He had just started his fourth trip down the stairs when Emma heard a crash. She ran to the top of the stairs and watched in horror as the front door burst open. River water gushed through. A log, carried by the great force of the current, had rammed against the door, breaking the lock.

Rob dropped what he was carrying, shouted, and fled back up the stairs.

"What was that noise?" Miss Clara asked, joining the children at the top of the stairs.

Emma felt paralyzed as she looked down at the swirling water and the big log that now blocked part of the doorway. Rob must have felt the same, for he pointed down at the log without a word.

"Oh, no," Miss Clara said.

The water lapped at the staircase until it reached about a third of the way to the top. Firewood floated and bumped against the walls.

"Let's get inside the front bedroom," Miss Clara said.

Somehow, Emma forced herself to walk the few steps down the hall to the room. Miss Ruthann's pale face stared at her, and then she turned back to the window.

"I knew it would come in this time," she said. "It hasn't flooded like this for thirty years, but I knew this time the river would take over."

"Well, it won't get this high," Miss Clara said. She added a piece of wood to the fireplace, and Emma shivered when she watched the orange-colored flames lick around the wood. The room was damp and cold now that the downstairs was open to the winter air and the icy river.

"I wonder if Father got his equipment to higher ground," Rob said softly to Emma.

Emma nodded, but she was full of her own worries. She wondered if her family was safe at home and if they were worried about where she was.

Miss Clara frowned at Rob's feet and then pulled open a dresser drawer. "Take off your shoes and stockings and put these on," she directed. She held out some women's stockings, and Emma giggled. Rob glared at her.

"I don't care," he whispered to her as he peeled off his wet socks. "My feet are so cold they're numb."

When his shoes and stockings were drying by the fire, Rob padded over to the window where Emma and Miss Ruthann were keeping watch.

"It'll be night soon," Miss Ruthann said.

The gray sky became still darker, and rain once again fell. The street below looked unreal to Emma, like something from a nightmare. She had never seen Plum Street under water. From their vantage point at the high window, she could see to Water Street and beyond to the channel of the mighty Ohio. Other two-story houses across the street looked like one-story houses, their first floors immersed in floodwater.

"It sure came up fast," Rob said.

"The current must have built up a dam of logs and brush downriver and then broken through," Miss Ruthann said. "That's happened before."

"Look," Miss Clara said in an awed voice and tapped on the

window glass. "Must be from Shantytown."

In the distance, Emma could see a frame house being swept down the churning rapids. She shuddered. Would the powerful Ohio destroy the Davises' house, too?

## CHAPTER 2

# The Waters Recede

"Don't worry," Miss Ruthann said. "Papa made this house good and strong. The Ohio won't move one brick of it."

Oddly enough, Emma believed her. Suddenly, she felt calm inside, as though they had nothing to worry about. Or was she still in shock? For the last half hour, every time she'd looked outside, she'd gasped at the sight. Now it was too dark to see anything but her reflection in the window.

Miss Clara had lit a lantern and settled in front of the fireplace. Now she was toasting cheese over the flames. When it browned and started to melt, she placed it on thick slices of bread.

"My father, my mother—" Rob started.

"Neither Anthony nor Patricia can get here until daylight, if then," Miss Clara said. "The current may still be too strong. You children might as well settle down for the evening. Here's our dinner."

"There's only been one other time it's gotten in the house," Miss Ruthann said. "That was when Papa hung the hook in the fireplace, just in case it happened again, so we'd have a way to cook upstairs. We were up here for two weeks until the water went down. We had soup every day. You should have thought of water, Clara."

"*I* should have thought of it! I was toting your keepsakes up the stairs. You should have thought of it." Miss Clara laughed. "We both should have thought of it."

Two weeks. Emma bit her lip; she couldn't stay two weeks with the Davis sisters. Surely Father and Uncle Anthony would come for them at first light.

"Shall I say grace?" Miss Clara asked.

"I'll say it." Miss Ruthann launched into a long prayer of thankfulness that they were all alive and well.

Emma ate her bread and cheese and immediately felt thirsty, but there was no drinkable water. All she had to do was step down a few stairs and she could get all the water she'd ever want—but it was filthy and smelled of outhouses and garbage.

The night wore on. Emma and Rob curled up in heavy quilts near the fire. Noises downstairs woke Emma several times, and each time she sat up in the darkness, wondering for a moment where she was. Then she realized debris and furniture were floating against the walls or the staircase. Miss Clara's snore, almost as loud as her laugh, was nearly as disturbing as the thuds that echoed from below them.

Late in the night, Emma awoke to find the fire nearly out. Something was different, something she couldn't put her finger on at first. Then she realized the rain had stopped at last. She got up to look outside and found that the clouds had moved away, leaving the stars twinkling in the dark sky. Moonlight reflected off the water that lapped against the houses, but the churning and swirling she'd seen earlier had calmed. Emma fed the fire a couple sticks of firewood and settled back on the floor.

"Rob! Rob!"

Emma was startled awake at daybreak. She sat up sleepily and watched as Rob rushed to the window and pushed it open.

"Father!"

"Thank the good Lord you're safe." Emma could hear the relief in the voice from outside. "I knew you'd be here. I knew you would be. Is Emma there with you?"

Emma got to her feet and joined Rob at the window. The two sisters crowded in beside her. Uncle Anthony was below the window in a rowboat!

"Good morning, Anthony." Miss Clara laughed. "Come to take these children home?"

"I suspect they've overstayed their welcome." Rob's father smiled up at Emma. "Your mother will finally be able to rest once she knows you're safe."

"Oh, they were both a big help to us yesterday evening." With attention to each smallest detail, Miss Ruthann related the story of moving their belongings upstairs.

While she was talking, Rob put on his dry stockings and shoes, and Emma combed her fingers through her tousled hair. The children walked to the top of the stairs. Emma hung back while Rob opened the door, but curiosity overcame her fear. The floodwater had risen to four steps below the second floor. Rob quickly shut the door again.

The bedroom was cold from the opened window, so Emma slipped on her coat as Rob put more logs on the fire. Emma cast a worried glance at the two old ladies. Now that it was time to go, she was having second thoughts. Could the sisters manage without them here? She looked at the window doubtfully. She wasn't sure she and Rob could get them out the window to the boat; somehow, she couldn't picture Miss Ruthann having the strength to hold on to a rope. . .and Miss Clara might break it.

"Rob?" came his father's voice from below the window.

Rob scurried to the window.

"I'll throw this up, and you can tie it to something that will hold." Rob caught the rope on the first throw and tied it to the bedpost.

"Will you be all right here?" he asked Miss Ruthann.

"We'll be fine if you keep us supplied with water and firewood," Miss Clara answered. "And maybe some food, too." She laughed.

"I'll bring you supplies every day," Rob promised.

"Thank you for dinner last night," Emma added politely. Then with a sigh of relief, she reached for the rope.

Climbing out the window and holding on to the rope at the same time was no easy feat. The sisters never could have done it. Emma struggled to wrap her legs around the rope and lower herself hand over hand, but her skirts kept getting in her way, and the palms of her hands burned. Rob's father held the other end of the rope and guided Emma's feet to the hardwood flooring of the rowboat. Then he reached up to guide his son down the rope. Once they'd untangled themselves, Rob's father hugged both children tightly.

"Thank God you're all right," Uncle Anthony said again. "Let's get you home, Emma, so your folks will know you're safe."

"It's got to be ten feet deep here," Rob told Emma four days later as their rowboat floated down Elm Street. The shingle that jutted out over Barnett's Mercantile was almost that high off the street, and only the tip of it was above the water. Emma looked up at it; if she'd wanted, she could have reached up and touched it.

"I can't believe it's so deep," she said.

A light snow started as Rob turned the boat onto Front Street.

A couple minutes later, they slowed the boat as they reached the sisters' dwelling on Plum Street.

"Ahoy," Rob shouted, and the Davis sisters waved from the second-floor window.

"What have you brought us today?" Miss Clara called once she'd opened the window.

"Fresh eggs," Rob answered. "Lower the rope." He caught the free end and tied it to the water pail. Miss Clara pulled the pail up. Emma rocked the boat as she crawled toward the bow. Yesterday Miss Clara had spilled a good portion of the water from the pail, and it had splashed on Emma. She wasn't going to risk that again. Her hat and coat were already getting wet from the snow.

"Is that Emma with you again?" Miss Clara asked as she lowered the now-empty pail.

"Yes, Miss Clara," Emma answered.

"She brought the eggs and milk in from the farm," Rob said as he untied the rope and knotted it around the basket of food Emma held. Once again Miss Clara pulled up the rope.

"Tie on the wood rug," Rob said. Once it was lowered, he filled it with firewood. "Do you need anything else today?"

"No, we'll be fine until tomorrow," Miss Clara said. "Thank you."

"We'll see you tomorrow." Rob paddled the boat toward Main Street.

"God bless you," Miss Ruthann called after them.

"I wouldn't want to be stuck on the second floor like that," Emma said. "It would be like living on a deserted island."

"Except they're not really alone. They see us and others from church every day," Rob said. "Father says this could last a couple of weeks, and I'm in charge of taking them supplies." This was the second day Rob and Emma had been allowed to take the boat out on their own. The first few days, the water had been too swift, but now that it was starting to recede, Uncle Anthony had turned responsibility for the Davis sisters' care over to Rob.

"It's weird seeing snow on water," Emma said. "It doesn't stick." She was almost eleven, and she'd never seen it snow on this much water.

Rob guided the boat through the whirl of white toward what was normally a busy wharf. "The flooded area's about a mile wide. That's a powerful lot of water to get downstream."

"Look there!" Emma exclaimed. At the public landing, three steamboats were tied to trees because the wharves were underwater.

"Father says there's too much debris in the water to travel, even for a steamship. See how fast the water's moving out in the channel?"

The cousins explored the flooded streets, with Rob occasionally calling out for any other stranded townspeople. No one answered. The eerie quiet was in stark contrast to five days earlier when shouting merchants, with every hand they could find, had been moving their goods to upper floors or higher ground.

"Look there!" Emma said again. Water poured into the fourth story of the steam mill. "How deep do you think the river is?"

"Maybe seventy feet in the channel," Rob said. She knew he was parroting what he'd heard his father discuss with the men of the families who were staying with them until they could return to their flooded homes. "Have you seen enough? We ought to be getting home. Aunt Kristen might be waiting on you to start back to the farm." Emma's mother wasn't really his aunt, but that's what he called her.

"I'm sure glad Mama's been letting me come see you again. After me being gone all night, I was afraid she was never going to let me go anywhere again. Those first few days, she'd barely let me out of her sight."

"Father says the flood of '32 will be remembered for a long time."

"It's the worst I've ever seen. But why do you live here and get flooded year after year? That makes no sense." Emma felt suddenly impatient with her relatives for putting up with this mess again and again when they could have lived on higher ground outside of town the way her own family did.

"Father can't build steamships and carry them to the river," Rob said defensively. "His yard has to be on the water."

Emma shrugged. "I'd never live here. It floods *every* year. It's never missed one year."

"We're used to it," Rob said. "And nobody drowned this year."

"Thank God for that," Emma said.

She knew Rob couldn't argue with her on that point; he gave his energy to rowing the boat back toward his house. When they got to the edge of the floodwaters, he jumped onto a sidewalk and tied the boat to a hitching post. He held the skiff steady while Emma climbed out, holding her skirts up so the hem wouldn't get wet and muddy. Rob carried the empty water pail, and Emma carried the basket on the quarter-mile walk to the Etingoff house.

The place was bursting with activity. Mama and Papa plus Emma's little brother and sister, Rob's sister and parents, and the two extra families filled the house with noise.

Emma described the flooded area to her mother.

"Anthony," Mama said to Rob's father, "do you remember the big flood a few days after we moved to Cincinnati? We were scared to death we couldn't get all our belongings moved out of the warehouse before the Ohio ruined them."

24

"I remember," Rob's father said. "We almost lost my dog."

"That dog was a pesky animal," Mama said. "And I think your new one might be just like him." She motioned to the window where Rob's little brown dog was whining to get inside.

Rob's father grinned. "We call him Jackson."

"Why did you name your dog after the president?" Mama asked.

"Reminds me who's in office." He laughed.

The grown-ups talked a few more minutes before Emma's parents rounded up their children. Rob stood on the porch with the others while Emma's father hitched the team to the wagon. Then they loaded empty egg baskets and milk containers.

"We'll bring more goods into town tomorrow," Mama said.

"Thanks for taking me with you," Emma called to Rob. "I'll see you tomorrow. And then pretty soon school will start up again."

Rob nodded and waved, but Emma could see from his face that the excitement of having extra people around was wearing off. She knew people were bound to get more irritable as the water slowly receded.

School, which both Emma and Rob loved and where they excelled, had been called off because homeless people were living there until the water went down and they could reclaim their homes—if their homes were still there.

Every day Rob and Emma delivered supplies to the Davises, and every day the walk to the boat got longer as the water receded. Now they could see through the Davises' opened front door that the water in the parlor stood about three feet deep. It took a longer rope to reach the water bucket. And the longer the rope, the more water Miss Clara spilled on Rob and Emma.

"It smells awful," Emma said.

"You get used to it," Rob defended his town. Emma saw him gag sometimes, but he never liked her saying anything bad about it.

After they'd made his delivery to the Davis sisters, he rowed over to the public landing.

"The steamboats are gone," Emma said.

"They've been running for several days now. Some will dock here later this afternoon." He maneuvered the rowboat to avoid a roof sticking out of the water. It was all that was left of a house that had finally caved in.

"You can see more floors of the steam mill," Rob pointed out.

"This place is a mess," Emma said. "It's going to take years to get all this cleaned up." She made a gesture with her hands that encompassed the entire downtown. "It might not be cleaned up in time for next year's flood. Our creek is already flowing normally." She always felt like the country was more in charge of nature than the city was.

"It'll be hard work, but we'll get it cleaned up," Rob said. He wound up the tour and took Emma back to his house, where Emma's mother, brother, and sister were waiting.

As their wagon pulled away from the house, Emma let out a tiny sigh of relief. Usually she and Rob got along well; sometimes she even liked arguing with him. She was always pleased when she could hold her own against him.

Rob was a year younger than she was, but now he was a reader ahead of her in school, much to Emma's annoyance. But if there was one thing Rob loved to do, it was read. He had read nearly every book in the school and quite a few that he had gotten from the public library. The more he read, the more their teacher gave him to read. There was no way Emma could keep up with him, what with all the chores she had to do around the farm. Sometimes it just didn't seem fair.

"Reading is the basis of knowledge," the teacher had said. "The more you read, the more you know. The more you know, the more you'll get out of life."

Emma agreed with the teacher. She liked feeling as though she could travel to faraway places in the books she read. And she liked arithmetic, too. Working with numbers made her feel as though she had a better handle on the world, as though by counting and tallying, adding and subtracting, multiplying and dividing, she could map out her life in manageable chunks. She had added up all the chapters in every book in the Bible, for example, and figured out if she read five chapters a day, she could read the entire Bible in one year. She was already about a third of the way through the Old Testament.

But Rob was more than halfway through, and he had begun the same time she did. She just never seemed to be able to keep up with him. She liked discussing religion with Rob, but he usually seemed to know more about the Bible than she did.

By the next market day, when Emma saw Rob again, the floodwaters had gone down fast. It was as if someone had knocked a big hole in a washtub, and *whoosh!* the water was gone. All that was left was a stinking mess. If before the place had the stench of sewer and stagnant water, now it was worse than ever.

Emma agreed to help Rob hand-carry supplies to the Davis sisters. He wore a bandana sprinkled with cinnamon oil around his neck to pull up over his nose when the smell got too bad, and he handed an extra one to Emma. She tied it on, and they started toward the Davises'.

As long as they were on the high sidewalks of the stores, which were covered with sand and silt, Emma was happy enough to walk along at Rob's side. But once they had to cross the street, she balked. Driftwood littered the streets, but that was the least of the problems; it could easily be carted away and burned. But caught among piles of broken lumber were the swollen bodies of dead pigs. Before the flood, they had prowled the streets and eaten the garbage of the town. Now the dead ones stank and were covered with maggots.

"I'm not going in that filth," Emma said.

"You've got to," Rob said. "I can't carry all this alone."

Emma set her basket and water pail on the sidewalk. "Then you can make a trip back here and get it. I'm not going one more step."

"Fine." Defiantly, Rob stepped off the sidewalk and sank knee-deep in mud and slime.

Emma just folded her arms and watched him. A girl had to have her limits.

CHAPTER 3

# The Snakes

"I should never have told Mama I didn't go with you yesterday," Emma said as she and Rob walked down Elm Street toward the Davis sisters' home. They both carried pails of water, and Rob carried a bag of lye soap and some scrub brushes from the shipyard. "Then she wouldn't have made me go today."

Rob just snickered. Emma knew he was glad to have her with him even though he was still annoyed with her for refusing to go with him the day before.

The streets were passable today, but only a lane wide enough for a wagon had been cleared of the silt and debris. Merchants were cleaning out their stores, but it was slow work, and great mounds of sand and mud swelled in front of the businesses. Rob and Emma stayed in the lane when they could and dodged two fires in the middle of cross streets where the carcasses of dead pigs were being burned. The stench was horrible.

Finally, they turned onto Plum Street. The Davises' front door was still open, since it wasn't possible to shut it yet. The river had deposited sand and silt and mud six inches deep, and although Emma knew Rob had spent two days shoveling sludge, there was still more. The sludge was piled in front of the house, but she'd heard Rob's father say they'd shovel it onto a wagon and take it to the low marshy area on the edge of town whenever he had free time and an extra wagon. Right now his equipment was in use at the shipyard.

"Good morning," Rob called.

Miss Clara opened the door at the head of the stairs. "Good morning, Rob. I'm glad to see you brought fresh drinking water."

"Yes, ma'am. And I brought Emma to help us, too."

"Many hands make light work." She laughed loudly as usual.

"Where do you want me to start?" Emma looked doubtfully inside the house. It looked like a hopeless task.

"We've got the sludge out of the kitchen," Rob said. "You can start scrubbing the walls in there."

With a heavy sigh, Emma went into the kitchen. Rob carried the water pails upstairs and then returned to the kitchen.

Emma got to work and, after a couple of hours, she had the cookstove cleaned. Of course, it needed a good scrubbing, but by nightfall the sisters might use it to prepare their evening meal. The place still smelled unbearable, but that wasn't going to change anytime soon. Emma wrinkled her nose. The musty, stinky odor would probably linger until the Fourth of July.

"Guess I'll go shovel the parlor," Rob said.

Emma giggled; it was such a funny thing to say when you thought about it. Her arms and shoulders ached from scooping the heavy mud and slime, but she felt a tired sense of satisfaction as she looked around the kitchen and saw the clean surfaces emerging from the silt.

Then Miss Clara let out a shriek. Something long and black flickered between her ankles. She grabbed a butcher knife from the countertop and held it high.

"Leave it alone!" Emma yelled.

"What's wrong?" Miss Ruthann called from upstairs as Rob

banged through the door.

"A snake!" Miss Clara screamed.

"It's not poisonous," Emma said. "It's a harmless water snake." She poked the end of a broom into the cupboard where the snake was hiding. "Maybe I can get it outside."

"Kill it, Rob!" Miss Clara squealed.

"It isn't hurting anything," Emma said. "I'll get it out. Do you have a bag we can put it in? I'll take it to the river."

"Kill it!" Miss Clara demanded in a stronger voice.

"There's no need to kill anything," Miss Ruthann declared, standing in the kitchen doorway. "That's an innocent snake."

"If I had a flour sack, I could put the snake inside and take it to the river," Emma said over her shoulder. She had not taken her eyes off the snake, which had now coiled around the broom handle.

"There's one in this cupboard," Miss Ruthann said. She made her way to another cupboard and tried to open the door. "It's swollen shut. Rob? Can you open it?"

Rob pried the door open and took out a soggy, stinky bag. He held the sides out so that Emma could stick the end of the broom handle in it and force the snake off. His face was white, and Emma gave him a tiny grin. She might be a girl, but at least she wasn't afraid of something as harmless as a snake.

Once the snake dropped into the bag, Rob twisted the top, and Miss Ruthann handed him a piece of twine she had gotten from the cupboard. Rob took the snake bag out the back door and laid it on the step. "All right," he said to Emma when he came back in, "you can take it to the river when we leave."

"Why don't you clean up that stove so we can have a fire?" Miss Ruthann was obviously used to being in charge. "Heat would help dry this place out. What about the fireplace in the parlor, Rob?

Can you build a fire in there yet?"

"I'll get right to it." Rob hurried out to the new woodpile, and after a moment, Emma followed him. They picked up armfuls of wood and some lighter twigs for kindling. Rob's father had brought wood yesterday, and other members of their church congregation had also brought firewood to replenish the Davis sisters' supply.

Emma spent a few minutes wiping off the hearth and the wooden mantle before Rob started a fire. Soon the *snap* and *crackle* of little twigs told them the fire was burning, but it took some time and a lot of smoke up the chimney before some of the larger, damp pieces of wood caught fire.

Emma had turned to go back to the kitchen when she heard Rob let out a startled screech.

"What is it now?" Emma asked him.

"Two more," he choked out.

"Two more what?" She followed the direction of his horrified gaze and saw two curled S-shapes twined around each other in the corner. "Oh, snakes. They must have been on the smoke shelf in the chimney."

"I'll get the sack," Rob offered and ran from the room.

"What is it?" Miss Clara appeared in the doorway.

"Another snake," Emma said, feeling it was better to tell a half-truth than mention that there were two. "It was in the chimney," she added quickly. "They go for closed-in spaces, so I'm sure that's the last one."

Miss Clara's eyes got bigger.

"We'll look in all the small areas as soon as we get these out," Emma assured her.

Miss Clara glanced nervously around the room and hurried upstairs.

Rob came back into the parlor, holding the snake bag gingerly at arm's length. He watched as Emma expertly poked at one snake until it wrapped around the broom handle.

"How do you know how to do that?" he asked.

"We have snakes at the creek. They're sluggish this time of year, or they'd probably be slithering all over this place instead of staying in the corner."

"Why aren't you afraid of them like most girls?" Rob asked.

"They're just animals, like rabbits or dogs," she said in a low voice, thinking of the secret she had never shared with anyone.

Before he untied the twine, Rob shook the snake down to the bottom of the flour sack and then held it open so Emma could drop the second snake inside. He repeated the same procedure for the third snake, then quickly retied the twine.

"I told Miss Clara we'd look in other tight places for any other snakes," Emma told him.

She was glad they'd carried so much furniture upstairs, but there was still a buffet in the dining room. Gingerly, Rob and Emma looked through the filthy tablecloths and doilies that were stored there, but they found no other snakes.

"These linens need to be washed, and we need to carry this buffet outside so it can dry in the sun," Emma said.

With Miss Clara's help, they wrestled the thing between them and got it out in the backyard. Miss Ruthann came down and said she'd stir the linen in the washtub if Rob would draw water from the well. He lowered the bucket and pulled it up. The water was a little murky, but Miss Ruthann decided it was fine for the laundry.

By lunchtime, Rob and Emma had hung out the washing, started a fire in the cookstove, and finished shoveling out the parlor. As soon as the group had eaten their bowls of soup upstairs in the bedroom, Rob and Emma returned downstairs to work while the sisters took a brief rest.

"We always lie down after lunch," Miss Clara said. "At our age, it's necessary."

Emma had never thought about needing a nap, but she thought she could use a little shut-eye herself after putting in a hard morning's work. She wanted to go to sleep and forget the flood had ever happened. If she could close her eyes, maybe the sludge that covered the floors, the streets, and the yards would disappear. She just wanted life to return to normal so she and Rob could go back to school. With a sigh, she pulled her thoughts back to the snakes.

"What about the cellar?" she asked Rob. "There are apt to be snakes hiding down there."

"I think that's the door over there." Rob pointed to a narrow door near the stove.

Emma opened the door and looked down into the darkness below. "We'll need a lamp," she said.

Rob lit a lamp and carried it to the head of the narrow stairs, but it did little to illuminate the cellar's blackness. One step down, two, then three. On the fourth one, she saw him step into water. He backed up one step and stooped down, holding the lamp in front of him.

"There's something in the water." His voice sounded thin and shaky.

Emma squeezed close beside him. Circles in the water showed that something had surfaced then submerged again. "More snakes?" she asked.

"I think so." He held the lamp out as far as his arm would reach, and Emma saw a snake's head, its two eyes yellow in the lamplight. Rob's hand shook so hard he almost dropped the lamp.

He grabbed it with his free hand and would have lost his balance if Emma hadn't pulled him back.

"Let's close this door." She didn't mind snakes in the daylight, but down here in the darkness, even she felt a little spooked.

They lost no time climbing back up the few steps to the kitchen, and Rob shut the cellar door.

"You can't catch that one with the broomstick, can you?"

"No, and that gap's big enough for a snake to come right through," Emma said, "but I think they'll stay down there. They'll be afraid of the light and noise up here."

Just the same, though, Emma grabbed the rag Miss Clara had used to clean the stove and stuffed it at the bottom of the door.

"We can't tell the sisters," Rob said. "They've been living with snakes here all this time. There's nothing we can do, except scare them."

"Or at least scare Miss Clara," Emma said. "Miss Ruthann seems able to stand anything." Miss Clara was certainly the stronger-bodied of the two, but Miss Ruthann was stronger when it came to taking things in stride.

"This room is looking good," Rob said glancing around the kitchen. "I'll get back to the dining room."

Emma went back to scrubbing the walls and cupboards with lye soap. At least the soap's strong smell drowned the mud's rotten smell.

By late afternoon, Rob and Emma had put in a full day's work. Miss Clara had come back downstairs, but her sister stayed upstairs.

"What a difference this day has made," she said. "We can cook supper down here. I can bake bread tomorrow."

"Except Mother told me to ask you to Sunday dinner," Rob said. "And she said she won't take excuses. She said that it was time you two got out of this house, and Father will pick you up at the usual time for church."

"Then we'll be waiting for him," Miss Clara said with a laugh. "I'll bake bread on Monday. You'll be back then, won't you, Rob?"

"Yes, ma'am," he said.

"You, too, Emma?"

"I'll ask Mama."

Miss Clara thanked them for their help and reminded them to take the snake bag off the back porch.

Rob stuck the bag in one of the water pails, and he and Emma carried it to the river, just a few blocks away. Emma carefully untied the sack, then shook it upside down. The snakes plopped into the water. She watched them swim away.

"If you hadn't been there today, I would have killed them," Rob said.

"Then I'm glad I was there," Emma said, "although I'm tired and ready to go back to the farm. Cleaning up after this flood is hard work." But she knew there was other work waiting for her at the farm, her own secret chores that no one else knew she did.

They started back toward Rob's house, again dodging huge piles of sludge.

"Look around," Emma said. "This will take years to clean up. Where are they going to put all this stinky stuff? They can't leave it here on the streets."

"Father's going to a meeting about it tonight at Dr. Drake's house," Rob said. "They'll decide how to get rid of it."

"Still, it'll take years," Emma said. "How can you stand living here in all this?"

Rob opened his mouth as though he were going to argue with her, but then he just sighed and closed it again. Emma felt a little guilty for picking a fight with him when he was so tired. Sometimes, though, she couldn't seem to keep her mouth from saying pointy little comments she knew irritated him.

"Father and Dr. Drake will know what to do," was all he said this time. "It'll get better."

But the next time Emma hitched a ride to Rob's house, she learned that it could get worse.

"Dr. Drake says cholera is in England," Rob told her. "It will reach the East Coast this summer. He's sure of it. And he says it's just a matter of time before it will come here."

"What's cholera?" Emma asked.

"It's a disease that can kill people in hours. Dr. Drake says someone can get it in the morning and be dead by night." Rob's voice sounded even more scared than it had when he saw the snakes. "And Dr. Drake says it's coming here. He doesn't know when, but it's coming here."

CHAPTER 4

# Rob's Opportunity

On Sunday morning, Emma went in the wagon with her family to church. She hadn't told anyone about the snake in the cellar, and the omission weighed on her. She'd even lied when she told Miss Clara there was one snake in the chimney when there were two.

It didn't help her conscience any that the sermon was about the Ten Commandments. It seemed to Emma that the preacher shouted extra loud when he got to the commandment about lying. Emma squirmed on the hard bench and looked down at the floor.

"If we all lived by the Golden Rule, we would have no quarrel with our neighbor," Preacher Wood said. "We would have no problems in Cincinnati over the flood cleanup. Everyone would help his neighbor in the same way that he would want to be helped if his own house had flooded. We all use the streets. Shouldn't we all help clean them up? We should help our neighbors; we should help our friends; we should help our enemies."

While the preacher talked about enemies for a while, Emma didn't listen. She turned her thoughts back to the Golden Rule. She was helping Rob with the cleanup work. Of course, Mama and Papa had told her to do it, but she was willingly helping, at least most of the time. Did that make up for the lying? If she were living in a house that had a snake in the cellar, would she want to know?

She finally decided that if there was nothing she could do about it until the water went down, she wouldn't want to worry about it. And the Davis sisters *would* worry if they knew, especially Miss Clara. Miss Clara was more afraid of snakes than Rob was. Was it really lying if she was hiding the truth for someone's own good?

But Miss Ruthann wasn't all that scared, Emma mused. Maybe she should confess to her, and Miss Ruthann could decide whether to tell Miss Clara or not.

Her attention returned to the preacher when she heard a collective murmur from the congregation, like the wind moving through the trees before a storm.

"Dr. Daniel Drake has told me that cholera breeds in filthy places," Preacher Wood was saying, "and our recently flooded areas are perfect places for it. He urges everyone to dispose of the sludge in the middle of the river. If it's dumped at the edge, it could wash back up on the banks." The preacher leaned forward over the pulpit and looked sternly at his congregation. "If we obey the Golden Rule, we'll all help each other get Cincinnati back to normal and lessen the effect cholera has on our town."

After the sermon, church members buzzed with talk of cholera. Emma heard one man say that cholera could kill someone in a matter of minutes. Surely that wasn't so.

As promised, the Davis sisters joined Rob's family for Sunday dinner, and so did Emma's family. Talk centered on the cleanup and the cholera epidemic in Europe. After dinner, Emma had a chance to speak with Miss Ruthann alone. She helped her to the parlor and made sure the others were still occupied in the other room. Then she confessed what she and Rob had found. Miss Ruthann listened to what she said, and then she stared at Emma a moment before she spoke.

"Well, Emma, Clara didn't ask you directly if there were any more snakes, so I reckon you did the right thing in not volunteering the information. But you also did the right thing in telling me. Now I can be on the lookout but not let on to Clara."

A load lifted off Emma's shoulders just as if someone had lifted a ten-pound harness off her.

Miss Ruthann smiled at her. "You've sure been good help to us with this flood. I knew it was going to be a big one."

While the adults talked, Emma and Rob sat on the porch and read some magazines Dr. Drake had left. Rob's father and Dr. Drake had been friends since they were boys. Uncle Anthony had told the children about the winter of the earthquakes and how Dr. Drake had shown him how to set up pendulums so he'd know when an earthquake was coming, although most of them came in the night when he wasn't near his pendulums. Dr. Drake was always doing experiments.

Now Emma and Rob looked at the medical magazines that were full of news from Europe about the cholera epidemic. Different doctors wrote about their views on how the disease spread. "You'll have to ask Dr. Drake what he thinks," Emma said. "I can't understand all these technical words."

"I think I get the gist of it," Rob said soberly. "But I'd like to talk to Dr. Drake."

It was several days before they had an opportunity to see Dr. Drake. First, they had to check on the Davises. When they looked at the cellar, the water had only gone down a foot.

Rob's and Emma's mothers joined the discussion at the cellar door. Aunt Patricia knew what to do. "We'll never get this place smelling better if we don't get rid of that water and all those rotting vegetables down there. Rob, take a pail to the outside cellar door and dip that water out. The place won't dry if we don't. And according to what Dr. Drake told Father, that's where cholera can breed."

That word brought fear to Emma's heart. She didn't know how people caught the disease. The articles in Dr. Drake's magazines had said it was not contagious, so it couldn't spread from one person to the next. So how could they know it was coming to Cincinnati if it wasn't carried by someone? It didn't make sense.

"Should we dump the water in the backyard?" Rob asked.

Emma didn't see how it could hurt. They still had mounds of sludge everywhere. Uncle Anthony had said that as soon as he finished at the shipyard, he'd bring the wagon and some men over. Then they'd take that stuff to the middle of the river like Dr. Drake suggested.

"Just dump it away from the house," Mama said.

Emma carried a bucket outside, and Rob lifted the heavy cellar door and propped it open. Water reached to the top step, so Rob stood in the yard and dipped his pail in. He handed it to Emma, and she emptied it a few yards away where the sun had dried out the mud, while Rob filled the second bucket.

"Watch for that snake," Emma warned him.

"I am."

After a while they traded positions, and Emma dipped and Rob carried the water off to empty it. The cellar wasn't a large area—maybe six feet long by four feet wide—but it held a lot of water. After an hour of dipping, they had only lowered the water by half, and the backyard was looking as if it had been flooded again.

"Maybe we ought to let the water sink into the ground before we do any more of this," Emma said, and Rob agreed.

"You two have been working hard," Aunt Patricia said when she checked on them. "We're going to wash curtains. Would you two take those magazines back to Dr. Drake? I said I'd take them today before we went back home."

Rob took the magazines from the mantel where his mother had put them out of harm's way, and he and Emma fairly skipped out the front door, relieved to be released from the cleanup work.

It wasn't far from Plum Street to Dr. Drake's house on Vine, and they found him on the front porch as he was about to leave to check on some patients.

Rob handed the magazines to Dr. Drake. "Father says thank you for letting him read them."

"What did he think?" Dr. Drake asked.

"He said we should all be working together to clean up the flood areas before the cholera gets here." Rob hesitated and then asked the question he and Emma had been discussing the last few days, "Can cholera really kill a person in a few minutes? I didn't read that anywhere in there, but I heard a man say it at church."

"Did you read these magazines?" Dr. Drake asked.

"Yes. I—I want to be a doctor when I grow up," Rob blurted out.

"Well, well." Dr. Drake leaned against the porch rail. "I was a bit older than you when I read my cousin's medical books and decided the same thing. That's one of the great advantages of this country. Our citizens can choose what they want to be. Rob, if you set your mind to being a doctor, you can be one. Anyone can be anything he wants."

"He?" Emma asked. "What about me?"

The doctor smiled. "I'm sure you'll make a wonderful wife and mother someday."

Emma frowned, but she bit back the words she would have liked to say.

"Rob, would you like to follow me on my rounds today to see what it's like to be a doctor?"

Rob looked at Emma, his eyes shining. Emma tried to swallow her jealousy.

"I'll have to ask my mother," Rob said. "We're helping with the cleanup at the Davises'."

"That's important. Why don't we do it next week, then? I'll talk to Anthony about it and let you know a good day."

"Thank you, Dr. Drake," Rob said. "And thanks again for the magazines."

The doctor smiled and waved them on their way as he carried the magazines into the house.

Rob leaped off the porch.

"Emma, can you believe that? I'm going to go with the doctor on his calls. This will be a good experience for me, you know, to help me become a doctor."

"Humph," she said. "I didn't know you wanted to be a doctor."

"I didn't either until a few days ago. It was just like it happened to Dr. Drake," he said with awe in his voice. "After I read the articles in his magazines, I thought that I'd like to help people get well. I'd like to stop the cholera from killing people."

"He didn't tell you if people died in minutes or not," Emma said.

Rob cocked his head. "No, he didn't. I'll ask him again when I go with him next week. Oh, I hope we're not in school by then. But Father would let me go anyway, since Dr. Drake is going to talk to him. This is too important."

"Well, it's not like you're going to be a doctor after you go with

Dr. Drake for one day," Emma said. "You could have asked my grandfather about the cholera. He's a doctor."

"I haven't seen him since I learned about it," Rob said. "But now I get to go with Dr. Drake. He's a very important doctor."

"So is Grandpa Schroeder," Emma said, feeling annoyed.

Rob nodded, but she knew he was barely listening. With one street to go until they reached the Davises', he yelled, "I'll race you!" He darted off, but Emma kept walking. Sometimes Rob could be so aggravating.

That afternoon they dipped more water out of the cellar. Rob had just changed jobs with Emma when she dipped a bucket, scooping a snake with the water. While the snake splashed around in the bucket, Rob ran in the house for a sack, and they poured the bucket of water, snake and all, into the sack. Water leaked right through, but the snake stayed in.

They were getting near the bottom of the cellar, and it was mighty dark inside. Rob went for a lamp while Emma scooped up more water. Rotten apples and potatoes came with the last few scoops. She put her hands down to fill another bucket when something slithered over her fingers. She yelped and jumped back, startled. Rob was just coming out the back door with the lantern.

"Get the broomstick!" Emma yelled. "There's another snake down here."

She waited until he returned, and then she grabbed the broom and snake sack from his hands. Rob descended the steps with the lantern turned up high, and Emma followed.

They thoroughly examined each cellar ledge and shelf. By the time they went upstairs again, they had captured three more snakes.

Emma heard Rob suck in a long shaky sigh of relief as they climbed the cellar stairs, and she smiled to herself. Rob might be the one who would get to be a doctor when they grew up—but he was still scared of snakes.

That night at dinner, discussion centered on Dr. Drake, who had spoken to Rob's parents about allowing Rob to accompany him on his rounds. Emma concentrated on her food, trying not to mind that Rob was doing something she wanted to do.

"I didn't know you wanted to be a doctor," Rob's father said.

"I do," Rob said. "I want to help people get well."

"A doctor in the family. . .our son a doctor. What do you think of your brother, Sue Ellen?"

"Dr. Etingoff," Sue Ellen said with a broad grin, "would you pass the butter?"

CHAPTER 5

# Following Dr. Drake

The day Rob had been waiting for finally arrived. School wasn't in session yet, so he didn't have to worry about missing it. And Emma had a plan. She hitched a ride into town with her mother, who was taking eggs and milk to the market. Her mother dropped her off at the end of the Etingoffs' street, and Emma marched up the sidewalk to Rob's doorstep.

"Don't you need to help at the market?" Rob asked when he answered the door. She didn't think he looked very happy to see her.

"No. Mama said I could come over here."

"But I'm going over to Dr. Drake's house."

"I know." Emma pressed her lips together and looked at him. A long silence stretched between them, and Emma raised her eyebrows.

She knew Rob was well aware of what she wanted, but he wasn't going to say it. He didn't want her along.

"Good morning, Emma," Aunt Patricia called as she walked into the parlor. "Come on in. You're here bright and early."

Emma smiled. Rob had no choice now but to open the door and motion her inside.

"Yes. I thought I'd be needed at the market today, but Mama said I could come on over here to spend some time with Rob."

"This is Rob's day to go with Dr. Drake."

"She knows," Rob said. "And I'd better get going."

Emma stood in front of the door and didn't move.

"Wait a minute," his mother said. "Emma, did you want to go with him?"

"Mother," Rob said in protest.

"I'd be honored to go." Emma smiled again. "Thank you for asking." She turned and headed back out the door, still smiling.

"What if Dr. Drake says you can't come?" Rob asked as he caught up with her.

"Why would he do that?"

Rob sighed. "Well, don't say anything. Just listen to him," he said as they approached Dr. Drake's home.

"I won't get in the way," Emma said. "You won't even know I'm there."

"Why do you want to go on calls with him? You said you could ask your grandpa to take you."

"Maybe I want to see what's so great about Dr. Drake."

"Humph." Rob led the way around Dr. Drake's house to the side entry of his office. He knocked and stood back as Dr. Drake opened the door.

"Rob, I've been looking forward to your visit," the doctor said. "Please come in."

Rob still looked angry, but Emma could tell he was struggling to hide his annoyance from the doctor. "Do you mind if my cousin Emma comes along, too?"

Dr. Drake smiled. "Hello, Emma. You're more than welcome to keep us company. Why don't you two look around? I'll be with you in a minute. I have a patient in my surgery."

He went into a separate room and shut the door behind him.

"What an odd place," Emma said. "It doesn't look like Grandpa

Schroeder's office. What are all these rocks?"

A glass-fronted display case held maybe fifty different rocks. One wall of the office was lined with bookcases, which held row after row of thick, leather-bound books. Emma walked over to the bookcase and examined them—medical books. So it was one of these that Dr. Drake had read when he was a little older than Rob and then decided to become a doctor.

In one corner of the room sat a large desk, and behind it stood a skeleton. Emma stared at it and then moved over to touch its hand. "Do you think this is real?" she whispered.

"Of course it's real. That's bone, isn't it? It sure isn't wood."

"I thought maybe it was animal bone carved in these shapes, but it's not. This person was alive. This is creepy. Why wouldn't they have buried him? Or her? This could be a woman."

"It is a woman," Dr. Drake said from the doorway.

Emma gasped, but Dr. Drake didn't elaborate. He ushered his patient to the office door.

"That core will keep growing. The skin on the outside is dead. Only thing to do is cut it off from time to time, or you'll find yourself walking as if there were a stone in your boot. You can do it yourself with a sharp razor, but you must be careful not to go too deep."

The man thanked Dr. Drake and left.

"You said it's a woman," Emma said, pointing at the skeleton. "Why is she here? Why didn't she get a proper burial? Mama says a person deserves a Christian burial."

"She was a. . .a derelict, an intemperate person."

Emma didn't understand, and from his wrinkled brow, she didn't think Rob did either. For once he spoke up before she could. "What does that mean?"

Dr. Drake hesitated briefly, then answered, "She drank a lot of alcohol. She didn't have any relatives to claim her body when she died, so it was given to the medical school."

"That's horrible," Emma said. Rob scowled at her.

"It's not horrible, although I understand why you'd think so." Dr. Drake didn't seem in the least insulted by Emma's frankness. "We can't learn about the human body's ills unless we know about the body. We need to see how the bones go together. We need to know how the organs function."

"But no proper burial?" Emma repeated.

"The Bible says ashes to ashes," Dr. Drake said. "Her body would decompose anyway. It was her spirit that mattered. She made a contribution to society in death by having her body be used for science."

He walked over to the skeleton and patted its shoulder bone. "I don't know her real name, but I call her Kristen."

"Kristen! That's my mother's name," Emma said.

Dr. Drake looked taken aback. "Well then, I'll have to change her name to Ruth." He turned to Rob. "This," he motioned toward the skeleton, "is part of observation in anatomy and physiology, and both studies are important in learning medicine. Next to God, a reliance on science and learning prepares you for the trials of life, and there are many in this profession. Do you think you are suited to be a doctor?"

"Oh, yes," Rob answered without hesitation. Emma knew he wasn't about to admit that he found the skeleton as distasteful as she did.

"Shall we go? I must call on Mrs. Heckel, who has a touch of the gout."

"What about these rocks?" Emma asked as she walked past the glass case.

"I have some of them because of the minerals in them. Others contain fossils. The ones on the top shelf are from an Indian mound."

"You opened an Indian mound?" Emma asked. "Isn't that like opening a grave?"

Dr. Drake considered the question for some time. "I suppose it is, although I didn't think of it that way when I excavated several mounds about fifteen years ago. Some of the mounds are thought to be a thousand years old, and I knew there could be a lot of history buried inside. Since farmers around here were plowing through the smaller ones, and even here in Cincinnati a street cut right through one, I felt the ones I excavated would have been destroyed anyway. The arrow points and beads over here," he motioned toward another shelf, "are from a mound."

"We have one on our farm," Emma said, "but we leave it alone."

Rob gave her another frown. "Do you have to sound so bossy?" he hissed in her ear.

"We won't need to go to the livery stable for my buggy," Dr. Drake was saying, as unperturbed as ever. "Mrs. Heckel lives only a few blocks away."

Rob walked beside Dr. Drake, while Emma trailed behind. All the streets had not yet been cleared of the sludge from the flood, so it would have been hard to get a team and buggy through some sections of town.

"This must be cleaned up," Dr. Drake said, motioning to the flood debris. "When the cholera comes, it will be concentrated in filthy areas."

The cholera. Every time she heard that word, Emma's heart pounded faster. From the articles she and Rob had read, it seemed to be an uncontrollable disease.

"How is it spread?" Rob asked. "Why will it be in the filthy areas?"

"I believe it's spread by poisonous, invisible flying insects. These insects breed in filthy areas, much like mosquitoes breed in marshy areas."

"Then one person can't give it to another person?" Rob asked. Emma was listening intently.

"No. It's not contagious. There's agreement among doctors about that. But there's disagreement on how it's spread. Still, I believe I'm right about the tiny insects carrying it and giving it to one person after another. I think the atmosphere has something to do with it, too. Reports from London say it's focused in the poorest areas where there is neglect and filth. And those most vulnerable to the disease are the intemperate, like Krist—." He glanced at Emma. "Like Ruth, my skeleton."

"Here we are," he said, stopping by a two-story house not unlike the Davis sisters' home. "Mrs. Heckel doesn't know you're accompanying me today, so you'd better stay out here until I ask if she'll permit observation." He went inside, leaving them on the porch.

In front of the house, great mounds of sludge dried in the spring sunshine. "They look like the Indian mounds," Emma said, "except they aren't as high. This place sure stinks."

"We haven't got the flood mounds in the Davis sisters' backyard dumped in the river," Rob said. "We have to do that before the cholera comes."

"Do you believe that part about tiny flying insects we can't see? That seems silly." Emma plopped down in a clear spot on the porch step. "I don't think we get to go in."

A moment later, Dr. Drake came back outside. A deep frown had

51

settled on his forehead. Emma jumped up and stood beside Rob.

"We're going to see how Mr. Washington's leg is doing," Dr. Drake said.

"What about Mrs. Heckel?" Emma asked.

"A fake practitioner has sold her some liniment. Probably snake oil!" he snorted. "The poor and uneducated can easily be sold strange medical notions, but I thought Mrs. Heckel was above that." He shook his head. "I constantly fight these quacks and imitators."

He set a brisk pace as he walked to his next patient's house. Rob and Emma were almost running beside the doctor, who took one step to every two of theirs.

"Stay here," he said when they arrived at Mr. Washington's home. "I'll see if you'll be allowed inside."

Emma sat on the step with Rob, but she popped up a moment later when Dr. Drake reappeared. "You may come in," he said.

There wasn't much to see. Mr. Washington's broken leg was covered with splints, and Dr. Drake was more concerned with the fever that came and went than with the leg. He prescribed a medicine that Emma had never heard of, and the trio left and walked back toward Dr. Drake's home.

"When will people stop dumping their garbage in the streets?" Dr. Drake asked as they sidestepped pigs that were rooting in the decaying matter. "We have dead animals decomposing here with rotting vegetables. Is it any wonder that the cholera will come?"

He continued giving a lecture about filth and the creeks and animal carcasses that filled Emma with an uneasy sense of foreboding. She'd seen Mill Creek in the fall and early winter when it ran bloody red from the pork slaughterhouses, but she hadn't thought about it as a problem, just as part of the seasonal cycle.

They were only a block from Dr. Drake's home when a young

man charged toward them from the other direction.

"Dr. Drake! Thank God I've found you. We need you at the river. A man fell overboard."

"Is the Humane Society there?" Dr. Drake asked quickly. Emma had never seen the Humane Society in action, although she'd heard of their daring rescues.

"Yes, they just pulled him out."

Dr. Drake broke into a run, and Rob and Emma raced after him. A few moments later, they reached the river. Several people surrounded a still form on the wharf. One man leaned over the drowning victim and pushed on his chest, then turned him on his side.

"Make way. Dr. Drake's here," the young man said, panting in gasps.

Dr. Drake knelt beside the unconscious man and took over the resuscitating procedure. Not even a minute later, the man coughed and vomited river water. Dr. Drake continued working on the man until he coughed again and caught his breath.

"He's breathing," someone yelled, and a cheer went up from the crowd that had gathered.

Emma wished she knew how to help people the way Dr. Drake did. She would have liked to save lives. If only she were a boy, then she could be like Dr. Drake.

Fifteen minutes later, the young man was walking around as good as new.

"I'm awfully thirsty," he said, and the others laughed.

Dr. Drake, Rob, and Emma once again started walking toward his house.

"He's a healthy specimen, and now that the Ohio is out of him, he seems fine," Dr. Drake said. "After I stop by home to see if anyone is waiting or there are any messages, I need to go over to the hospital to see some patients, and you won't be permitted to go in there."

At Dr. Drake's house, they went inside while he collected some old issues of medical magazines for Rob to read.

"When you return these, we'll talk again," Dr. Drake said.

They were almost to the door when Emma turned back.

"Dr. Drake, is it true that a person can catch the cholera and be dead in a few minutes?"

"No," he said emphatically. "Not in a few minutes. However, records show that death has come as soon as six hours after an attack."

CHAPTER 6

# Independence Day

Rob and Emma together read the magazines Dr. Drake had given Rob, but since they were old issues, there was no mention of cholera in them. The issues of the magazine Dr. Drake edited, the *Western Medical and Physical Journal,* covered more than diseases and their causes and cures.

"How do you come up with all these writings?" Rob asked Dr. Drake when they returned the magazines for another pile.

"Studies," Dr. Drake replied. "I want to see how Western medicine differs from Eastern medicine, but I can't just give my ideas. I have to observe and then write down my conclusions."

"What kind of studies?" Emma asked. The way Dr. Drake looked at her made her fear she had been too bold in asking.

"You're a curious girl, aren't you, Emma?" His voice sounded as though he wasn't sure if that was a bad thing or a good thing.

"I'm curious, too," Rob put in, but Emma wasn't sure if he was defending her or trying to shift Dr. Drake's attention back to himself.

Dr. Drake looked at him and smiled, and this time, the approval was written clearly across his face. "That's a good thing, Rob. That curiosity is going to take you far in life." In a low voice, as if musing aloud, he added, "You need direction, but you're too young for formal training." He walked over to his desk and sorted

55

through a drawer, taking out a pencil and some paper.

"Rob, how would you like to help me with some scientific experiments?" he said as he drew some lines on the top sheet of paper.

"Oh, yes!"

Dr. Drake wrote some more, then looked up. "Here's what you do. Each day I want you to record the temperature of the air at your house, then down at the river. You'll need a thermometer. Do you have one?"

"No."

"I'll order one for you next time I need supplies."

"I've seen one in Barnett's Mercantile. Maybe Father would get it for me."

"I imagine he would. Anthony has a curious mind, too, and he'd want to foster that in you. And what about you, Emma?"

"Me?"

"Yes, you. You have a questioning mind and an outspoken tongue." Dr. Drake chuckled. "It's clear to me that you want something out of life—but you'll have to work hard to get it." Again his voice was so low that Emma wondered if they were supposed to hear. Dr. Drake's soft words filled her with a prickly feeling of excitement. She was willing to work hard.

"Now, there are a few other studies you two could do for me," Dr. Drake said in a louder voice. "One is to notice the clouds at two times each day and record the type. The times must be consistent—the same. And when you go to the river to measure the air temperature, you must leave the thermometer in the same place for a few minutes to get an accurate reading. Don't leave it in direct sunlight. While you're waiting, measure the depth of the river. Use the flood gauge at the public landing and record the direction of the wind, and the speed, too, if you can."

With school starting up again after the flood cleanup, Rob made a schedule of when he and Emma could record their observations. That way they would be consistent. Rob's father bought him a thermometer, which he kept in a leather pouch so it wouldn't break when they carried it to the river each morning before school. At that time, they measured the river depth and looked up at the sky. After school, they again measured the river depth and recorded the type of clouds and where they were in the sky before Emma went home and Rob went to the shipyard to do his regular cleanup work. With the threat that cholera would come to Cincinnati, Rob's father was a fanatic about keeping the place free of garbage.

"Why do you think Dr. Drake wants all this information?" Emma asked.

"I think so he can see if the temperature affects any events that occur. Dr. Drake said the cholera is affected by the atmosphere, but I'm not sure about the river. Maybe he wants to see if the temperature affects the height of the river."

At home on the porch, Rob showed her a book he had checked out of the library that had all types of clouds in it. "Those are storm clouds there," he said and pointed to the sky.

Emma looked at him as if he were crazy. "Of course they're storm clouds. Everybody knows that. It'll be raining in a few minutes. The breeze has cooled down, too."

Rob whipped his thermometer out of its leather pouch and set it against the porch rail. He sighed. "Why do you always have to act as though you know more than me?"

"I don't. But sometimes I do know more than you. Should I just keep quiet?"

Rob didn't say anything, but Emma thought she read his

answer on his face. After a moment, Rob said, "You know the saying: Red sky at night is a sailor's delight. Red sky at morning, sailor take warning."

"Sure. I know that, too."

Rob sighed again. "Well, Dr. Drake says we can prove that by scientific observations. If we record the look of the sky in the morning and the sun shines pink and red on the clouds and later it rains, and that happens over and over in the same way, then we can draw a conclusion that when the sky looks like that, it will rain later in the day."

"We didn't have a red sky this morning," Emma said.

"No, it doesn't mean we will always have a red sky before we get rain, but if there is a red sky, it will probably rain."

"We'll see. I might start some of my own observations out at the farm."

"Dr. Drake would like that. He has doctors in other parts of the state making observations, too. He says next we'll record the different plant life, to see if it has any effect on things."

As spring moved toward summer, Emma was busy helping her parents around their farm, but she also spent more time with her scientific observations. She measured the distance around the big oak tree that grew in the middle of the pasture, and some of the other trees, too, but she recorded these numbers every week, not daily. She measured the height of the wild rose bush that grew beside the henhouse. She counted blossoms on one limb of the redbud tree and recorded the length of time that passed before the pink blooms fell off. Then she measured the tiny puckered leaves every day, and soon they were full-grown, flat, heart-shaped leaves.

"You are a natural scientist," Dr. Drake told her when she showed her notebook to him.

Emma felt her face turn pink with pleasure.

"What about you, Rob? Are you keeping records as well?"

"I want to be a doctor," Rob said.

"You will be someday, but first you must understand the world God gave us and what change brings what result."

After that, Rob kept his own notebook full of observations.

Each week the temperatures on Rob's and Emma's charts climbed. Then summer arrived, and plans were made for the big Fourth of July celebration.

"After the parade and speeches," Emma's mother said a couple days before the event, "we're all going to the Etingoffs' house. Anthony will fetch the Davis sisters. You and Rob can set up the big table in the yard before the parade. Then we'll use all the quilts to sit on. Anthony is going to bring some lumber from the ship-yard so he and Rob can put together some benches."

"Why do we always make such a fuss over the Fourth of July?" Emma wondered out loud.

"It's right that we celebrate this holiday with family and friends in this great nation," Papa said.

"Are you going to give a speech?" Emma asked.

Her father looked surprised. "A speech? No."

"You sound like a speech maker." Emma waved an arm out as if gesturing to a crowd. "In this great nation," she mimicked her father's deep voice.

Papa chuckled. "I guess I sound like a politician, when I'm just a proud American. This country gives us freedom. Freedom to speak what we feel, freedom to worship as we believe, freedom to become anything we want."

"Dr. Drake said that, too. He said I can be anything I want to be as long as I set my mind to it." Emma was pretty sure he'd been talking to Rob when he'd said that, but she'd taken it to heart anyway.

"He meant you can be anything as long as you're willing to work for it. And you're going to want to take good care of your own home one day. You're a good worker, Emma." Papa gave Emma's hair a gentle tug. "I know you're going to be a wonderful wife and mother."

It was hard to sleep that night. Emma's bedroom was hot and stuffy and she lay awake thinking about what Papa had said. Why couldn't anyone understand that she wanted to be something exciting when she grew up, the way Rob wanted to be a doctor? Rob would probably be a husband and a father one day, but no one talked as though that was the only thing he should be thinking about when he looked toward the future. Why should things be any different for girls?

She sighed. At least she had her secret. Even if no one else knew what she was doing, *she* knew.

The Fourth of July dawned with no red skies. *It will be a good day,* Emma thought as she downed her oatmeal in big gulps. They left for town early, and as soon as they arrived, Emma and Rob raced to the river to make their morning recordings.

When they returned, they helped carry the big table to the yard. Mama set her pies on one corner and covered them with a cloth to keep the flies out.

"This is to keep you out, too," she told Emma and Rob with a laugh.

By late morning, they stood on the side of the street, watching the Independence Day parade. Hundreds marched by them, waving. Some men represented trade associations. Children marched with their Sunday schools. A festive air surrounded them all as the nation's freedoms were celebrated.

"Do you want to listen to the speeches?" Emma asked.

"Maybe one," Rob said, "if it doesn't go too long."

"Politicians always speak too long," Emma said, but she walked with Rob to the end of the parade route where the speaker's stand had been erected. The first speaker had the crowd's attention, and roars of approval filled the air as he punctuated every accolade for the United States of America with his fist in the air. But after an hour, Emma was tired of standing and listening, and she was hot and hungry.

"Want to go home now?" she whispered to Rob so she wouldn't upset those around them who were listening to the orator.

He nodded.

They edged their way out of the crowd, then headed toward home. Under the shade trees in the backyard, they found the Davis sisters visiting with their mothers. Emma's three-year-old sister, Mary, lay on a pallet sound asleep. Her little brother, Timothy, played with Rob's dog, Jackson.

"Are the speeches over?" Mama asked.

"No. I think they'll go on for a while," Emma said. She drew some cool water from the well, drank a dipperful, and then handed the dipper to Rob. "Listening to how great this country is sure makes a person thirsty."

"It was probably the hot sun and not the words," Mama said.

Over two hours later the others arrived in separate groups. First Rob's grandparents arrived, then Emma's grandparents, and then more cousins. The backyard was filled with laughter and talk until the women uncovered the food.

"Let us thank God for the providence He's given us," Rob's father said. The others stood and bowed their heads.

"Thank You, our heavenly Father, for the joys of this day. We live in the greatest country in the world because we are free. And the greatest freedom we have is to worship You in any manner we choose. Please guide us to make choices that will please You. And bless this food to our bodies that we may be stronger and serve You better. In Jesus' name, amen."

"Amen" echoed through the gathering.

The adults filled their plates from the large table. Then it was the children's turn to heap fried chicken, cornbread, green beans, and boiled potatoes onto their plates. After they'd eaten all the pies, someone called out for some music, and Mama retrieved her harmonica from the wagon.

She called out, "What's your favorite?"

Miss Clara named a tune, and Mama jumped into the song. Others sang along and called out more favorites. After a while, Papa and Uncle Anthony lit lanterns and placed them among the group.

It was well after dark when Mama finally put her harmonica away and the group broke up.

Emma helped carry empty baskets to the wagons lined up in front of the house. Rob's father escorted the Davis sisters to a wagon and left to take them home. The others bid farewell into the night. Emma's family was the last to leave.

"Thanks for the hospitality," Mama called to Aunt Patricia.

"Another great Independence Day," Rob said to Emma. "The best country in the world—where we have freedom. We can all be anything we want to be as long as we set our minds to it."

"Not all of us," Emma said as she climbed onto the wagon.

"What's that supposed to mean?" Rob asked.

But Emma turned her face away and didn't answer.

CHAPTER 7

# News from New York

With the big Fourth of July celebration over, Emma settled down to helping her parents on the farm, but she still had time to record her scientific observations—and whenever she could catch a ride into town, she visited Rob. He might aggravate her sometimes, but he was still her best friend.

"Have you seen Dr. Drake this week?" she asked one hot mid-July day. "I thought I'd see if I could borrow a book from him."

"A book on what?" Rob asked as he finished sweeping the floor of his father's office.

"I want to know more about the bones in his skeleton."

Emma thought Rob gave her a funny look, but he only shrugged and said, "Let's go see him."

Together they walked toward Dr. Drake's, but they met him on the street a block from his home.

"It's here," Dr. Drake said in a solemn voice. "The cholera is in New York."

Emma's stomach did a strange little flip. Now the dreaded disease wasn't just something that was spreading in Europe and that she read about in magazines. Now it was in the United States. How long until it reached Cincinnati?

"When will it get here?" she asked.

"Hard to say. Could be a few weeks, could be a few months.

We must get people to clean up the filth here. We must get rid of the breeding places for the cholera."

"How did it get across the ocean?" Rob asked.

"Must have come on a ship. The report I have from a doctor friend in the East is rather sketchy." He held up a letter. "The disease reached New York nearly a month ago."

"A month?"

"Yes. There's no time to lose. I'm on my way to talk to some of the Board of Health members. The city must take precautions. We must ensure the safety of our citizens." He raised a hand in farewell and marched on down the street.

Rob and Emma stood looking at each other.

"It's here," Rob said, echoing Dr. Drake's words. "We must warn the others."

They ran back to the shipyard. Emma could feel her heart pounding in her chest.

The moment Rob saw his father, he yelled, "The cholera's in New York."

His father dropped the hammer he was holding. "Who told you that?"

"Dr. Drake. He thinks it came on a boat."

"Then it will probably come here the same way." Rob's father looked toward the Ohio River. "Every boat should be inspected before it's allowed to tie up at the wharf. If there's sickness on it, it can't stop here. I'll go talk to Dr. Drake."

"He's not home. He's talking to some Board of Health members."

"I'll find him. Go tell your mother."

Rob and Emma raced home. As soon as they broke the news to Rob's mother, they headed for the marketplace to tell Mama. The news spread like wildfire through the market.

At the dinner table that night, Papa prayed, "Our heavenly Father, thank You for this day and this food. Please deliver us from the pestilence of cholera that's in New York. . . ."

Emma didn't listen to the rest, but she added her own fervent prayer to that of her father's: *Please, God, don't let the cholera kill my family.*

"Anthony says Dr. Drake has called a meeting of all interested citizens tonight," Papa said. "I'm going to hear what he has to say."

"Can I go with you?" Emma asked.

Papa looked at Mama, then shook his head. "You'd better stay here. I'll tell you what he says when I get home. Or maybe tomorrow. It may be late when I get back."

Emma went to bed and watched the stars out her window. She could hear the mantle clock *tick-tock, tick-tock* in the parlor below her room, and still Papa didn't return from town. What could they be discussing this long? She fell asleep dreaming that the invisible cholera insects hovered over Cincinnati.

At first light, Emma awoke and rushed downstairs. She smelled coffee and found Mother and Father in the kitchen.

"What did he say?" Emma demanded.

"The afternoon newspaper will have a full report," Papa said, "in case I forget something. Mostly what Dr. Drake said was that we must clean up the marshy areas where the disease can breed. We must clean out cellars and air them. Garbage must be disposed of properly so it won't make our drinking water impure. It's up to the citizens to clean up this town. The Board of Health doesn't have any money to hire people, so we have to do it ourselves. There are places where the flood sludge hasn't been properly disposed of. These are the breeding places."

Emma's mouth formed a large *O*. "Nobody got the big pile out of the Davises' backyard," she said.

Papa looked at Mama. "I'll take the wagon into town and talk to Anthony. You can come along, Emma."

"I'll air out our cellar," Mama said. "Timothy can help me carry things out."

When Emma and her father arrived at the Etingoffs', Emma and Rob ran to the Davis sisters' house. They told them of the coming disease and the plan to remove the dried sludge pile in their backyard.

"I didn't want to say anything about it," Miss Clara said, "but I did wonder about it."

"We'll take care of it. And we'll make sure the cellar is dry," Rob said.

Emma knew Rob didn't want to go down into the cellar, just in case they had missed a snake when they were draining the place. He opened the outside door and then hesitated at the top of the stairs. Emma pushed by him with a lantern held high and descended the steps into the gloominess. A musty, rancid smell made her nose wrinkle. The dirt floor was still muddy, and puddles of water stood in every hollow. She looked around for snakes, but all she saw were spider webs hanging in the corners.

"It's still wet," she said as she went back up the stairs. Rob nodded and went to tell the sisters.

"We'll keep the outside door open during daylight hours," Miss Ruthann said. "A few days ought to dry it out. When does Dr. Drake say the cholera will come?"

"He doesn't know. He just says it will come."

On Sunday, the minister commented on the flurry in Cincinnati as townspeople cleaned up the garbage in the streets and aired out cellars.

"But it isn't enough for you good people to take care of your own. You must reach out to those less fortunate and help them. Down by the river is an area of filth that must be taken care of."

Emma knew where the pastor meant. She and Rob had passed near it when they went to the river to measure the depth, but both of their mothers had warned them to stay away from the squalor and degradation of that area. Now she was filled with curiosity.

"Let's go see for ourselves," she whispered to Rob.

Later that afternoon, the two children walked purposefully to the edge of what could only be described as a shantytown. Men sat outside small clustered shacks and drank liquor. Women cuddled up beside them. Dead animals rotted in the gutters. Garbage stank in the hot sun.

"My mother would skin me alive if she knew I was down here," Rob said.

Emma nodded. "I just wanted to see what the preacher was talking about. This sure is a place where the invisible cholera insects could breed."

"It's the stink that's the worst," Rob said. "Let's get out of here."

The children quickly marked down their observations in their notebooks, then hurried back to Rob's house.

A few days later, Emma was back in town on market day. She was to deliver some fresh eggs to the Davis sisters, but she had walked by Rob's house early that morning to accompany him to measure the river.

"Let's walk by the shantytown again," she said.

"There's probably nobody there," Rob said. "They'd be working today."

But they weren't working. Even so early in the morning, groups of men, with a few women here and there, sat around on crates. The stench was as great as it had been on Sunday—maybe worse, as more fly-covered garbage had been added to the stinking piles around the shacks.

"Why are they here?" Emma asked.

"Maybe they don't have jobs," Rob said.

"They could come to the country and farm. There's land enough for everybody. Don't they know that?"

"Hey, whatcha got there?" a rough-looking man hollered. He staggered toward them so unsteady on his feet that Emma thought he must be sick.

All Rob held was his pencil and the paper he made his daily observations on, and he quickly stuffed them in his pocket. Emma stuck the small basket of eggs for the Davis sisters behind her back.

"Gimme those, girlie," the ruffian demanded and grabbed Emma's arm.

She screamed and dropped the basket. Rob jumped on the man, but the burly fellow shook him off. With the basket in his grip, the man turned around, and Emma yelled, "Run!"

With Rob close on her heels, she raced down the street away from the shantytown. She could still hear the awful man's boisterous laughter follow them.

They didn't stop running until they were two streets away from the shantytown.

"Are you all right?" Rob asked when he could catch his breath.

"Yes, but Mama's going to be mad about that basket. And what will I tell Miss Clara about her eggs?" She shook her head. "That thief got a bunch of broken eggs. I dropped that basket hard."

"You shouldn't have gone over there again," Rob said.

"You shouldn't have come with me if you thought it was such a bad idea."

"I couldn't let you go alone. It wouldn't be proper for a girl."

"A girl! I'm nearly a year older than you, Rob Etingoff, and I know how to take care of myself just as well as you do."

The argument would have continued because Emma was just warming up, but when they turned down another street, they saw a commotion a couple blocks away. A crowd was gathering.

"Smoke!" Rob yelled. Spirals of black curled toward the sky.

"The hotel!" Emma shouted as they raced down the street.

Men and women alike poured out of nearby buildings. Many carried buckets, and one man yelled above the roar of the crowd, "Form a line! Start a brigade!"

Rob and Emma joined the ranks of townspeople who stretched in a line to the river. A couple of men filled buckets and handed them to the head of the line. At first, Rob had to carry the bucket twenty feet to Emma, but soon others filled in the gaps and the sloshing buckets changed hands quickly. Another line had formed to the closest brick cistern, but it soon ran out of water, and the line shifted to another cistern. The fire was raging. From her place in line, Emma could see flames on the roof and hear windows shattering from the heat.

Emma's shoes were wet. Her skirt was damp and stuck to her legs. But the cold river water that spilled on her felt good in the early August heat. She glanced at Rob, who was working as hard as she was, passing the full buckets toward the hotel and passing the empty buckets back toward the river. Further down the line, she saw Papa and Uncle Anthony and the men from the shipyard all working as fast as they could to move the buckets along. The entire town had turned out to help put out the fire—but they didn't seem to be making any headway. At least the wind wasn't blowing. There was hardly a breeze. It hadn't even moved Rob's wind scale that morning when they'd recorded the reading.

Within two hours, the hotel had burned to the ground. Thanks to the townspeople's tenacity, the buildings around it hadn't caught on fire. They had doused them with water once they saw there was no hope of saving the hotel. Now the lines disbanded and groups milled around while the charred remains of the building continued to smolder and send thin wisps of smoke heavenward.

Emma and Rob hurried to join their fathers, who stood in a group with some other men.

"We've got to do something about it," Papa was saying. "We could patrol the areas at night, since most of the fires occur then. It's odd someone could start this one without being seen, but from the way it went up, it had to have been set."

"Someone set the fire?" Rob asked.

"It appears that way," his father said. "It started at two different ends of the hotel. That's mighty suspicious. Hard to believe that two accidental fires could start at about the same time in the same hotel."

"The sawmill went up the same way," Papa said.

"And that steamship," another man added.

"There's definitely an arsonist on the loose," Rob's father said. "And now there's one more area to clean up before the cholera comes."

## CHAPTER 8

# Cholera!

More fires were set through August, even though a volunteer group including Emma's and Rob's fathers patrolled the downtown area at night. Emma and Rob watched the elegant Pearl Street House burn to the ground, but they heard rumors that it would be rebuilt. Two more steamboats burned, and then it seemed the arsonist had done all the damage he wanted. By September, the volunteer arsonist control group disbanded without ever catching the arsonist, and the men were home again at night.

Life settled into a new routine as school started the fall session. Mama had sprinkled chloride of lime in the yard, the cellar, and the outhouse as part of her cleanup and as a possible deterrent to the cholera. Emma got the white powder on her shoes every morning when she walked out to the wagon to go school. Then she left footprints wherever she went.

Of course, the stuff was spread in other places, too, since many townspeople thought it would keep them safe from the cholera. Emma saw a few areas where it was dumped on top of garbage instead of the garbage being taken to the middle of the river.

Rob and Emma continued their practice of going to the river twice a day to measure the depth and record the air temperature, the cloud formations, and the wind direction. The skies had never been brighter nor the air as clean as on a late September afternoon after school when Emma and Rob stood on the wharf making notations.

They watched a steamship approach and dock. There wasn't the usual activity aboard. Something was odd. A man wearing a captain's hat scurried off the boat and looked about in a frantic manner.

"Hey, boy!" he called out.

"Me?" Rob answered, pointing a thumb at his chest.

The captain came quickly to his side and said in a quiet voice, "We need a doctor. Can you fetch one?"

Emma gasped. "Is it the cholera?"

The captain ignored her question. "Can you get a doctor?" he asked Rob.

"Yes. I'll be right back," Rob said. Both children ran as fast as they could to Vine Street. "Dr. Drake, Dr. Drake!" Rob yelled the entire block before they reached the house.

Dr. Drake met him on the porch.

"Rob, what's the matter? You could raise the dead with that kind of shouting."

Rob glanced first one direction, then the other. "I think the cholera is here," he whispered. "A steamboat captain has asked for a doctor."

Dr. Drake turned white, then laid his hand over his heart. "God help us through the soul-trying days ahead. Take me to him. Then I want you to run as fast as you can away from there."

"But you said we couldn't catch it from other people."

"That's true. But we don't know where the invisible insects may be."

When the children and the doctor got to the river, no one from the ship was on land. But as soon as they clomped onto the wooden wharf, the captain appeared on deck and disembarked again.

"I'm Dr. Daniel Drake. What is it? The cholera?" the doctor asked without waiting for the captain to identify himself.

"We need to bury three, and two more are ill."

"We are as ready as we'll ever be," Dr. Drake said with a sigh. "I have a pesthouse set up, and the red flag is ready. I'll get a wagon."

The captain returned to the ship, and Dr. Drake looked off in the distance, then down at Emma and Rob.

"Go. Go quickly. Now! Go!" With each word, his voice grew stronger, and the children turned and ran. Emma was sweating in the September sun, but at the same time she was shivering.

When they were a block away, she tugged on Rob's elbow and pulled him behind the corner of a building. "Let's see what Dr. Drake does," she whispered.

They waited for Dr. Drake to return with a wagon. A few minutes later, Emma saw the victims being taken ashore and placed in the wagon. It rumbled off in the opposite direction from their hiding place. She didn't know where the quarantine house was, but she'd heard talk that no one wanted it near them, so she suspected it was on the edge of town. Maybe it was even near her own house.

Rob's father would know. "Come on!" she hissed in Rob's ear, and together they raced to the shipyard. When they saw Rob's father, Rob didn't yell his news this time. He whispered it in a voice that was filled with the fear.

"Dr. Drake just took two people from a steamboat to the pesthouse. Three more are dead."

"The cholera?" His father's voice was quiet.

Rob nodded.

"Go tell your mother, and stay at home the rest of today." He turned to Emma. "You need to find your father and get on home."

"But what about the sweeping up?" Rob asked.

"Go on home. Go!" Emma heard the same urgency in Uncle Anthony's voice that had been in Dr. Drake's.

They started walking back to Rob's house, but they had only gone a few yards when they both quickened their steps. Without a word between them, they were suddenly running. They rushed inside the house, and Rob slammed the door behind them.

Sue Ellen poked her head from the kitchen doorway. "What's wrong? You both look like you've seen a ghost."

"We've seen cholera," Rob said.

"Cholera?" Sue Ellen seemed to choke on the word. She turned back into the kitchen. "Mother. . ."

"Where is it?" Rob's mother demanded in a low voice as she walked toward Rob.

"Brought in on a ship, just like Dr. Drake predicted. He's taking two people to the pesthouse."

Rob's mother sat down hard on a chair in the parlor. "We need to warn the others. Did you tell Father?"

"Yes, he sent me home and said to stay here."

"All right. Get the lime and spread it in the yard and on the street in front of here. I'm going to tell the Davis sisters and warn the preacher. Emma, you stay here until your father gets back from the market."

Once his mother left, Rob got the bag of chloride of lime, and Emma helped him sprinkle it outside. Would it kill the invisible cholera insects? she wondered. Or would it keep the vapors that attracted the insects from forming? Dr. Drake had mentioned that atmospheric conditions affected the spread of cholera. But it was a beautiful Indian summer day outside. How could there be any disease in this clear air?

"I'm scared," Sue Ellen said when they went back inside. "What do we do? Can we go to school tomorrow?"

"I don't know," Rob replied.

At supper, Papa prayed for the safety of Cincinnati, then shared his news from the quarantined house.

"Dr. Drake has treated everyone on board the steamship with calomel, and the ship has anchored near the Kentucky side of the river. The dead have already been buried and all their belongings burned."

"What's calomel?" Emma asked.

"A laxative. It makes you go to the bathroom," Papa explained. Emma made a face.

"Dr. Drake says the disease feels like poisoning," he continued. "A person's insides hurt something fierce."

"Can we go to school tomorrow?" Emma asked.

Mama and Papa exchanged a glance, and then Mama said, "We are not going to panic about this. Perhaps Dr. Drake can isolate the cases and it won't spread. You can go to school, and we'll wait and see what happens."

"It's not contagious," Emma said. "It can't be spread from one person to the next. Dr. Drake is certain of that."

"It seems awfully strange to me," Mother said. "I don't understand how invisible insects can cause it. Wouldn't the insects be carried by one person to the next? Isn't that what contagious means? Like smallpox?"

Emma wasn't sure herself, but she had heard Dr. Drake speak to this question many times, and she quoted his words. "Once you get smallpox, you can't get it again. But you can catch cholera over and over."

"Then why have the pesthouse?" Mama asked.

Papa answered that one. "It's so the townspeople won't panic. So that they feel there is something being done. Dr. Drake had a hard time finding a building, and the one he got is rundown. But it will serve the purpose."

"Where is it?" Emma asked.

"On a side road, just outside of town."

On Sunday, the preacher led the congregation in prayer and then preached about the cholera as a divine imposition.

"This plague is a punishment from God's own hand," he boomed. "It is a scourge to the thoughtless and immoral among us. Those who have weakened themselves by intemperance and living in filth have called this punishment on themselves.

"There have been four deaths in the squalor down by the river," he announced, and the congregation gave a collective gasp.

Emma caught Rob's eye. "We need to talk to Dr. Drake," she whispered. Her parents usually ate Sunday dinner with the Etingoffs. After she and Rob recorded their daily observations, they could walk over to the doctor's house.

"We will observe our own day for prayer and fasting since President Jackson will not declare one for the nation," the preacher continued. "On Wednesday our congregation will lead the way by fasting and praying to avert the cholera."

Over Sunday dinner, Sue Ellen asked why the president wouldn't help the nation get over the cholera.

"That's not exactly what the preacher meant," her father said.

"President Jackson wouldn't declare a day of prayer because he thought that decision should be left to churches. Our country was founded on religious freedom, and I believe the president was right in keeping government and churches separate. We don't want another church's beliefs forced on us. We won't tell other churches when to have a day of prayer, and they sure can't tell us."

Discussion followed about the cholera and what could be done about it. After his second piece of blackberry cobbler, Rob pushed his chair back and said they were going to record the observations.

"You don't need to go to the river," his mother said. "I thought Dr. Drake wanted your observation reports as something to do with the cholera coming. Well, it's come." She sounded angry, as if the reports were supposed to stop the cholera, and they hadn't.

"Father?" Rob appealed to his other parent. "I won't go near Shantytown. I promise."

His father looked at his mother, while Emma's parents looked at each other. Emma could read their answer on their faces. "I don't think you need to measure the river today." Mama's voice told Emma there was no point arguing.

"However," Rob's father said, "I'll go with you if you want to talk to Dr. Drake."

How had he known what they wanted to do? Their wonder must have shown on their faces, because Uncle Anthony said with a grin, "I want to talk to him myself."

"And so do I," Papa said.

They called on Dr. Drake at midafternoon, but he wasn't there.

"He must be at the pesthouse," Rob's father said. "Let's go see if Miss Ruthann's feeling better. Then we'll see if Dr. Drake's home."

The Davis sisters had not gone to church with them that morning. Miss Ruthann had fallen a couple of days earlier, Miss Clara had told Uncle Anthony that morning when he had gone to take them to church, and she was feeling poorly. Miss Clara hadn't wanted to leave her sister alone.

"Ruthann's resting in bed," Miss Clara said, once they were seated in the parlor. "She's not doing very well."

Emma glanced around the room. Pictures hung on newly whitewashed walls, and the furniture shone with polish. Who would have guessed that six months ago this room had been underwater?

"Is there anything she needs that we could bring her?" Rob's father asked.

"She's partial to apples," Miss Clara said.

"I'll bring in some early apples on market day," Emma offered.

"That would be real nice of you, Emma," Miss Clara said.

They visited a few more minutes, and the children and their fathers walked back over to Vine Street.

Dr. Drake still wasn't there, but they sat on the porch and waited, and within a few minutes, Emma saw the doctor's horse and buggy down the street. Rob's father pushed himself off the porch step and walked out to the street. The others followed.

"We heard there were four deaths by cholera in Shantytown," Anthony said before Dr. Drake could even climb down off the high seat.

"That was by yesterday evening. There were eight more today."

"Eight more?" Rob asked. "Eight?"

"And I have seven severe cases in the pesthouse. I'm going back there in a few minutes."

"It's spreading fast," Emma's father said as they walked to the porch.

"Yes. The invisible cholera insect is breeding at an alarming rate. I can almost see them hovering above that filthy area." Dr.

Drake leaned against a column on the front porch. His features were drawn, and he looked as if he hadn't slept in days.

"You can see them?" Emma asked.

Dr. Drake closed his eyes a moment before he answered. "No. In my mind I can see them, and when my eyes are open, I can imagine them as a vapor rising from the filth and garbage. I'm afraid they won't long be content to remain in that area."

Rob's father cleared his throat. "I know that you said this isn't contagious, but it's hard to convince people of that. Patricia is fearful. She's covered our yard with lime, and she doesn't want Rob and Sue Ellen to go back to school. Our family outside the city feels the same way."

Emma and Rob looked at each other. They hadn't known their mothers were thinking of keeping them away from school.

"Fear is a powerful emotion," Dr. Drake said. "It could predispose a body to be attacked by a malady."

A frown formed on Anthony's forehead. "Are you saying that if a person is fearful, she has a greater chance of getting the cholera?"

"Any violent emotion could weaken a body's constitution," Dr. Drake said. "And fear is one of the strongest emotions."

"They wouldn't let us go to the river to make our observations," Rob said. "They're awfully afraid of this."

"I imagine they're afraid not for themselves, but for their families," Dr. Drake said.

"But the fear is still the same debilitating emotion. Is that right?" Father asked.

Dr. Drake nodded. "What are you thinking, Anthony?"

"I'm going to send my family out of Cincinnati. To the country," he said. "Rob, how would you like to spend a few weeks on the farm with Emma?"

CHAPTER 9

# Country Life

On Monday morning, Rob, Sue Ellen, and their mother packed their clothing and some bedding, and their father loaded up the wagon. They arrived at the farm before lunchtime.

Emma felt a satisfied sense of having been right about something before even the grownups had figured things out. Just a few days before, she had said to Rob, "How can you stand it in town with the cholera around, the thieves and fires and floods and filth and pigs everywhere, and the smell? You'd all be better off if you lived outside the city where we do."

She practically saw Rob's hackles rise. "I notice you always make it to town for the Independence Day parade. And when the circus came to town last year, you were there. And you always hang around after school and after church. You've been pretty fond of the library lately, too, ever since Dr. Drake got you so interested in bones and such. So if Cincinnati's such a bad place, why don't you just stay away?"

Emma had put her nose in the air. "I'm not saying Cincinnati's all bad. I'm just saying that the country is obviously a safer and healthier place to live. I'd think you could see that."

But Rob had refused to see reason. Emma grinned at him as he climbed down from the wagon, but no answering smile softened his face. Instead, he looked grim and discouraged, as though coming to stay with her family was some sort of terrible imposition.

Mama came out of the house and stood next to her on the porch. "I'm so glad you're here," she said to Rob and his family.

"We hate to put you out like this," Rob's mother said.

"You know you're welcome here anytime for as long as you like," Mama said. She reached for a valise. "What's happening in town? Anything new this morning?"

"People are dying right and left," Aunt Patricia said. "Rob, take this bag." She turned back to Mama. "I couldn't rest easy with the children in school and the cholera lurking who knows where."

"The fresh air out here is just what you need," Mama said. "I'll put you and Anthony in the front bedroom."

"I'm not staying," Rob's father said. "But I'll be back on Sunday when the shipyard's closed."

"Anthony, is it safe?" Mama looked worried.

"I'll be fine. My men need their pay for their families, so we have to keep the shipyard open. We've spread lime all around the yard, so we'll be fine." He smiled reassuringly at Rob's mother.

"Well, come on then," Mama said. "Let's get you settled. Then we'll at least have something to eat before you go, Anthony. Or can you stay until tomorrow?"

"No, I've got to get back."

They carried their belongings inside and gave the horses water. Then Mama fixed the noon meal. As soon as Papa came in from the far pasture and they had eaten, Uncle Anthony hitched the horses to the wagon and headed back to town.

Patricia stayed on the front porch until he was around the big curve out of sight. Emma saw her wipe away a tear before she took a deep breath and smiled at Rob and Sue Ellen. Her lips looked tight, though, as if she were fighting to keep them from trembling.

"Father will be okay, won't he?" Rob asked.

"He'll be fine. He said he would, and he will," his mother said. "And every minute he's away, I'll implore God to help Anthony keep his word." She took another deep breath and turned toward the front door. "Let's see if we can be of help to Kristen."

But there wasn't much for the Etingoffs to do. "Emma did the morning chores already, before you got here. You can help her tomorrow morning," Mama told Rob. "If you'd like, the two of you can walk down by the creek. Maybe take measurements like you did in town."

That sounded like a good idea, so Emma and Rob took their pencils and notebooks and walked down to the creek. Sue Ellen tagged along for something to do.

They walked through a field where dead cornstalks crackled in the breeze, then through a brushy area, and finally to the creek. It wasn't a river, and it couldn't compare to the mighty Ohio, but Emma had always liked the gurgling sound the water made as it rushed around an area of built-up rocks, the place where they always crossed the creek.

"We need a good place to do a measurement," Rob said in his I-know-more-than-you-do voice. "It has to be the same place each time." Emma watched him pick up a long stick and gingerly step near a steep bank where the water flowed by only a foot from the top. There was no flood pole to use as a measure, so he stuck the stick in the water. It was deep here, at least deeper than the three-foot stick he'd found. He lay down on the bank and wagged the stick around, thrusting his hand into the cold water, but the stick still didn't touch bottom.

"I need a longer stick. Maybe a pole." The water was deceptively clear but deep. He looked around under nearby trees, but he couldn't find a stick that was strong enough and long enough for his measuring stick.

Echo, Emma's pet crow, fluttered down on her shoulder. Emma stroked his breast with a finger and then shook her head at Rob. "I already have a measuring place. We don't need another one." With Echo still clinging to her shoulder, she showed Rob the huge chestnut tree downstream whose trunk was submerged in the water.

"The creek's eaten away the bank on this side, so I measure how high or low it is from this notch on the bark." She pointed her finger. "This is the normal height. Right here."

"Right here," Echo mimicked.

Rob looked like he would have liked to argue, but what could he say? "Your bird talks?" he asked, changing the subject.

"He fell out of a nest as a baby, and I fed him worms and milk until he was stronger," she said proudly. "Echo repeats what I say."

Echo was just one of the many things about the country that was better than the city. Surely, even Rob would see that now. "The cholera won't come out here," she boasted. "We don't have the filth you have in town."

"Why do you have to remind me?" he asked in a low voice. "I hate thinking about my father and Dr. Drake being in the city with the invisible cholera insects."

His words made Emma feel guilty. "I wish you could see the insects," she said. "Then people could swat them, smash them, and kill them so they wouldn't harm anyone. How can people fight something that's invisible?"

At supper that night, Rob's mother said, "We want to make ourselves useful, Kristen. What can we do tomorrow to help out?"

Mama and Patricia discussed the work that needed to be done around the farm. Then Mama turned to Rob, "And you can help Emma with early chores by gathering eggs."

Emma helped Mama make a pallet for Rob on the floor of the front bedroom. His mother and Sue Ellen shared the big bed. Both families gathered for a good-night prayer, and Rob whispered one of his own for the safety of his father and his friends in Cincinnati. Emma felt guilty again for being so impatient with him. He couldn't help it that he had grown up in town—and he certainly couldn't help being born a boy while she was a girl. In her heart, she said a prayer of her own and asked God to help her be kinder to her best friend.

Before daylight the next morning, she tiptoed into the front bedroom and gave Rob a nudge on his shoulder. He didn't move, so she gave him a shake until he groaned and clutched the pillow over his head. "Time to get up, sleepyhead," she whispered. "You're supposed to help with the eggs this morning. Father will take them to market tomorrow."

Rob nodded and dressed quickly. In the kitchen, he took the basket that Mama handed him.

"We appreciate your help, Rob," she said as she put a piece of wood in the cookstove. "Emma, you show him what to do, and then you can do the milking. I'll have breakfast ready when you finish chores."

Emma and Rob walked to the henhouse, Emma holding a lantern in front of them. During the day, the hens ran loose in the yard, but at night they were closed in to roost. The door squeaked as she opened it, and the hens clucked at the disturbance.

"You just shoo the hens off the nests and collect the eggs," Emma said. "It's not hard." She set the lantern down and pointed at the first nest on the side opposite the door. "Go ahead. You do that side, and I'll do the other."

Emma kept an eye on Rob as she collected the eggs from her side of the henhouse. The hens made a racket, but they ambled off the nests, and Rob collected several eggs. But the fourth hen he tried to move must have awakened on the wrong side of the nest. She wouldn't budge when Rob poked at her. Instead, she pecked him—and Rob jerked his hand back with a yelp. He tried it again, and she pecked him again, harder this time.

Emma bit back a giggle, and Rob glared at her. "I'm bleeding!"

"Want some help?"

Rob shook his head. "I can do it," he said between his teeth. He moved on down the row. "I'll come back for the tiger chicken."

He successfully ousted all the other hens except the reddish-colored one that had pecked him. A few hens milled around the room, and others returned to their nests. He tried to move that grouchy hen again, and she attacked. She ruffled her feathers and flew at him. Rob yelled and stepped back, narrowly missing the lantern. He threw his arms up to block the hen—and hurled the basket into the air. The eggs plopped down on the ground, every one of them broken. The hen landed and pecked at Rob's shins. He pushed past Emma and ran outside, slamming the door behind him.

Emma pushed the door open. "Are you okay?"

He nodded, looking shamefaced. "I'm sorry about the eggs."

"I'll clean up the mess," Emma told him. "Old Red can be moody. I should have taken her side of the henhouse."

"I'm sorry," Rob said again to Papa when he came in from the barn.

"It's no matter. There will be more eggs tomorrow before I go to town."

And there was no shortage of eggs for breakfast. Mama and Patricia had fixed smoked ham, potatoes, eggs, biscuits, and ham gravy, and the children ate their fill.

"We have a surprise for you children," Mama said as she set four lunch buckets on the table. "You're going to school. We got permission for you to attend the country school. Mr. LaRose is the teacher, and he said you are welcome to come as long as it's unsafe for you to go to town school."

Emma and Rob looked at each other. Emma wasn't sure if this was a good thing or a bad thing, and she could tell Rob wasn't sure, either.

Mama laughed. "Go on with you now. You would have been bored doing chores around here all day, and you know it."

So Sue Ellen, Emma, Rob, and Emma's younger brother, Timothy, set off for the one-room schoolhouse a couple of miles down the road.

## CHAPTER 10

# The One-Room Schoolhouse

Above the autumn-colored leaves of the trees, Emma could see the peak of the belfry on the little one-room schoolhouse. She'd been here before for harvest suppers and other community gatherings, but not for school. The line that divided the town school district from the country school district was the western property line of her parents' farm. Emma's next door neighbors went to the country school, while she went to school in Cincinnati.

It felt funny to be going to school here. But she knew Rob and Sue Ellen felt even stranger, so she marched down the road and into the small, dusty building as though she didn't have a qualm.

Mr. LaRose stood at the front of the room behind the desk. He was a little man with a deep frown line between his eyes. It got deeper when he looked at Rob and Sue Ellen. "I don't know you."

Emma made introductions.

"We don't know how long we'll be here," Rob explained. "When the cholera is gone, we'll go back to Cincinnati. Maybe next week," he said, but Emma knew that wasn't likely.

"I suspect there will be more who flee from town before you get to go back," Mr. LaRose said. "Take a seat, please, everyone."

Emma glanced around and saw that there were several other students, some younger and some older than she. They all shuffled into the seats, clattering the connected desks.

"All right then," Mr. LaRose said. "Let me hear how you read." He had Sue Ellen read from a book and then Timothy. "You two may stay seated next to each other," he said. "You read at the same level."

Mr. LaRose took the book and moved down the aisle. "Your turn," he said and had Rob read a section. "You're very good." Mr. LaRose had him read from a more advanced reader, then another. "Sit in the back with the older boys." Mr. LaRose pointed with his ruler.

Rob slid onto a bench in the back as Emma began to read. She was eager to prove to Mr. LaRose that she could read as well as Rob, but in her nervousness, she stumbled over a few big words. "All right then," Mr. LaRose said when she had finished the paragraph. He moved her back a few seats behind Timothy and Sue Ellen, but not as far back as Rob. Emma's face felt hot as she took her seat.

Mr. LaRose pulled the bell rope, and the clanging brought a few more chattering students inside. Emma's neighbor two farms down sat next to her; she watched as a tall, lanky boy of at least fifteen sat down by Rob. Another boy, this one burly, sat on his other side.

"Who are you, Shorty?" she heard the tall boy ask.

"Rob Etingoff from Cincinnati."

"I think *Shorty* fits you better," he said.

"I'm not short. I'm just not as old as you."

"Oh yeah?"

Emma stopped listening to the conversation behind her as the teacher tapped his long stick on his desk.

Mr. LaRose wrote on the board and started different sections of the students on assignments. Then he turned his attention to the younger children and their sums.

When Mr. LaRose finally got to the back half of the room, he passed out books to Rob and Emma and gave the older students reading assignments. When everyone had finished, he asked them to help the younger students with their reading. Emma immediately claimed Sue Ellen and Timothy, and Mr. LaRose nodded his approval at her.

At noon, the four cousins sat on the schoolhouse steps in the sun. Emma pulled out some biscuits and cheese and apples from her pail, and she handed out portions to her brother and Sue Ellen and Rob.

"Hurry and eat, and we'll go play prisoner's base with the others," she said.

Some of the students had stayed inside to eat, and others were also eating their meals outside. As soon as they were done, they organized the game.

"I'll be on Benjamin's team," Rob said, pointing to one of the boys who had sat beside him.

"You don't get to choose," the other boy said. "The captains choose their teams."

"In my class, we get to play with who we want to," Rob said.

"Well, this isn't your class," the boy said. "And that's not how we do it here."

"Hey, Shorty, you're on my team," a boy named Patrick said.

"My name's Rob."

"Right, Shorty," Patrick said.

Emma shot Rob a sympathetic look as she ran away with her own team.

Children of all ages darted every which way, running from members of the other team to keep from being tagged.

"Where's our territory?" Emma asked.

"Our base is the pine tree," a girl named Luanne said.

"But where's—"

"You're caught," Patrick yelled as he tagged Emma on the back. "I'm taking you prisoner." He pushed her toward his team's base, the well.

"I don't even know the territories yet," Emma said. "You can't come into our safe area."

"We don't have safe areas," Patrick said. "That's not the way we play."

"In school in Cincinnati we play this different. We have—"

"We're not in Cincinnati," Patrick said. "Stay here until someone rescues you."

Emma stayed put, but inside she was seething. Maybe it wasn't going to be much fun going to school here in the country after all.

Luanne darted to the well and slapped Emma's shoulder. "You're free. Run."

"Don't we have to count to ten before we run?"

"What? Run!" Luanne shouted.

Emma stood still with her hands on her hips. "But at my school, we—"

"This ain't your school," Luanne said over her shoulder. "Run!"

Before Emma could move, Rob ran in and tagged Emma. *He seems to be learning the new rules just fine,* Emma thought sourly.

"You're still a prisoner," Rob yelled.

"You're not playing fair!" Emma shouted. "At our school in Cincinnati—"

"Time out!" Patrick yelled.

Everyone stopped, and all eyes turned toward Patrick, who marched over to Emma. Sue Ellen and Timothy edged toward Emma, but everyone else seemed to be lined up against her, even Rob. She had never felt so alone. *It's not fair,* she thought. *This is my territory. I live just down the road a couple of miles. Their way doesn't make sense, and they should listen to me. It's not like I'm a city kid like Rob. . . .* Her thoughts trailed away in a jumble of anger and frustration.

"This ain't Cincinnati," Patrick said. "If you want to play, you play by our rules."

Emma glanced at Rob. He was looking at her with sympathy in his eyes—but he was standing next to Patrick.

"We play it differently," Emma said. "Don't we, Rob?"

Everyone's eyes turned toward Rob, but he was silent for a long moment. Emma felt her face grow hot. Surely, at least Rob would take her side. . . .

"Their rules aren't so bad, Emma," Rob said at last. "They're just different. You've just got to pay attention and listen. You'll catch on."

"Don't talk to me like I'm Sue Ellen's age," Emma said between her teeth. Suddenly, she'd forgotten about Patrick and Luanne and all the others. This conflict was between her and Rob alone, and it had bred from countless other fights over the past few months. She realized the two of them had both been struggling for the upper hand—and neither one of them was ready to give in.

Before their face-off could escalate, Mr. LaRose rang the bell, calling the students back to class. Emma glared at Rob and headed inside.

"This afternoon we'll have a spelling bee with the whole school," the teacher announced.

"How can that be fair?" Emma whispered to Luanne.

"Emma Farley, do you want to say something to the school?" Mr. LaRose asked in a gruff voice.

Emma flushed. She'd never been reprimanded for talking in class before.

"Well?"

"I—I was wondering if the younger students would be given the same words as the older students."

Mr. LaRose stared at her. "Of course not. The words will be according to the age of the speller." The teacher divided the students into two teams, and they lined up on opposite sides of the room.

"The first word is *hat*. He wore a hat into the barn."

"H-a-t." The youngster spelled it correctly.

Mr. LaRose turned to the other side of the room. He gave out words that fit the different abilities of the students. Then it was Rob's turn.

"Your word is *quarantine*. The boy was placed in quarantine."

Rob pronounced the word, then spelled it correctly. Emma thought it didn't hurt that he'd seen that word over and over in Dr. Drake's medical journals.

Mr. LaRose went through the students again. A few misspelled their words and had to take their seats. Emma's word was *embargo*. She spelled it successfully.

Within a few minutes, only three students were left. Patrick and Emma were on one side of the room facing Rob on the other side.

Patrick missed *desert* by putting in an extra *s*, which made it *dessert*, and he had to sit down.

"Your word is *monthly*," Mr. LaRose said to Rob. "He pays a monthly payment to the bank."

Rob spelled it correctly.

"Emma, your word is *renowned*. He was a renowned writer."

"Renowned," Emma repeated and then hesitated. "R-e-n-o-u-n-e-d," she spelled.

"That's incorrect. Rob, spell *renowned*. He was a renowned writer."

"Renowned. R-e-n-o-w-n-e-d."

"Correct," Mr. LaRose said. "You both may be seated."

The teacher didn't say one word to Rob about being the winning speller. Instead, he started a geography lesson for all the students.

"I think we'll change Shorty's name to *Smartypants*," Patrick whispered in a voice loud enough for the whole room to hear. Emma hid her smile.

By the end of the day, Emma had had enough of the country school, and Rob looked like he had, too. But Mr. LaRose wasn't through with either of them.

"Rob, you can take your turn today sweeping out the schoolroom." He pointed a gnarled finger at Emma. "And you, Miss Farley, can clean the blackboards."

Emma looked at Rob, but he only shrugged and went to get the broom.

"You're both very smart children," Mr. LaRose said when they had finished their chores. "But you need to learn to adapt to your situation."

"What do you mean, sir?" Rob asked.

"You're smart enough. I'm sure you'll figure it out before tomorrow. Talk it over between the two of you."

Emma and Rob put on their coats and went outside. "I wish I was home," Rob muttered as they went down the steps. "What do you think is going on there today? How many people do you suppose have died?"

Emma didn't have an answer. She was just glad the day was over. An unspoken truce stretched between the two cousins, and she sighed. As angry as Rob made her, he was still the person she knew best in all the world. Being with him felt so comfortable, like wearing familiar old shoes instead of her Sunday shoes that pinched her toes. With Rob, she always knew that even if she made him mad, even if he made her mad, they still understood each other.

When they got home, they walked to the creek and measured the depth. There was no change. As a matter of habit, Rob also recorded the cloud formations and looked at the weather vane on the barn for the wind direction. But he had one more thing to say about the day's experiences before he could let it go.

"I don't like Patrick. When Mr. LaRose was busy at the other side of the room, he called me *Smartypants*," he told Emma as they walked back from the creek.

"Smartypants!" she said.

"Smartypants! Smartypants!" the crow on her shoulder echoed.

"Well, you *are* pretty smart." She looked at his trousers. "I don't know that your pants are smart, though," she said and laughed.

"That's not funny," Rob said. "I hate that school. Don't you?"

Emma shrugged. "It's just so different from what we're used to. I expect we'll get used to it."

Rob scowled and kicked a rock on the path. "I hope we don't have to. I want to go home."

The next day, Rob collected the eggs, except for the one under Old Red. Emma got that one for him—and she didn't say a word to tease him. Then both children trudged to school with the others.

The day went more smoothly. Even Mr. LaRose seemed more relaxed, and the cousins were getting used to their new school.

Later that afternoon when Papa returned from the market, he wasn't alone. Miss Clara Davis sat on the high bench of the wagon beside him.

Emma and Rob were outside when they drove up.

"Miss Clara?" Rob asked. "Where's your sister?"

"Ruthann died of the cholera," she said and broke into tears.

## CHAPTER 11

# Dr. Rob

After Miss Clara's announcement, Emma ran behind the henhouse and cried. Miss Ruthann had always been so kind. She could hardly believe that from one day to the next, the old lady had died. When she returned to the house, the family was grouped around Miss Clara as she sat in the parlor. Tears streamed down her face, and Mama's and Aunt Patricia's eyes were red. Rob had his head down, but Emma could see that he was brushing away his own tears.

"Can you talk now?" Patricia asked at last. She held Miss Clara's hand tight. "When did this happen?"

"Monday evening." Miss Clara's voice was thick. "That morning a peddler came around selling apples. Ruthann's been wanting fruit, so she asked me to get her some, and I did. She wasn't strong at all, and after she ate the apple, which was a little on the green side, the cholera attacked her. She died before sunset." A fresh burst of tears ran down Miss Clara's cheeks.

"Does Anthony know?" Patricia asked.

"Oh, yes. I sent for him straight away when she got sick. He brought Dr. Drake, but it was too late to move Ruthann to the pesthouse. We buried her yesterday. Anthony thought I should come out here, and Thomas brought me." Miss Clara glanced at him with grateful eyes.

"Well, you're welcome to stay here as long as you'd like," Mama said. "I think we should have a service for Miss Ruthann before we have our meal. Thomas?"

"It would only be fitting," he said. While he got the family Bible from a parlor table, Mama fetched her harmonica from the bedroom.

She played a hymn, and then Papa talked about the blessings of God and the glory of life in the hereafter, where Miss Ruthann now resided. Patricia spoke about Miss Ruthann's goodness, and Mama remembered times when she was young and Miss Ruthann had helped her with sewing.

"She always talked to me at church," Sue Ellen said. "And she gave me the chicken leg when she'd have Sunday dinner with us."

Emma wanted to say something, too. She had so many memories of the wonderful old lady. "We found a snake in the cellar, but we couldn't get it out because the water was high down there. Miss Ruthann said it was okay that I didn't tell Miss Clara, but she was glad I told her so she could keep an eye out for it."

"There was another snake!" Miss Clara exclaimed. "Why didn't she tell me?"

Miss Clara sounded so much like her old self when she used to argue with Miss Ruthann that Emma couldn't help but laugh out loud.

Once she started, she couldn't stop laughing. At first, she felt embarrassed, but then Mama joined in, and then the others. Miss Clara's loud laugh sounded almost natural. After the laughter died down, Emma felt better, almost as if Miss Ruthann was still among them.

"Miss Ruthann's probably looking down here today and laughing with us," Mama said.

Papa read a verse from the Bible about ashes to ashes and dust to dust, the family prayed together, and then the service was over.

"When we go back to Cincinnati, you must show me where she's buried so I can put flowers on her grave," Patricia said.

"I will." Miss Clara's eyes were filled with tears again, but she blinked and walked with her head high to the kitchen. "Anything I can do to help?"

Emma noticed that Rob didn't seem to feel any better. His eyes were sober, and his lips were screwed up in a tight little bunch, as though he were still trying not to cry. He touched his mother on the arm to get her attention.

"Do you think Father will be all right?" he asked in a low voice.

"Don't worry, son. He'll be fine." But Patricia's tight smile told Emma she didn't quite believe her own words. "We'll keep praying for him."

Rob nodded, and then he slipped outside. From the window, Emma saw him heading toward the woods. She thought about joining him, but something about the set of his shoulders told her he wanted to be alone.

The next morning, Emma and Rob gathered the eggs together. Emma clucked at Old Red and sneaked her hand to the side of the chicken. Then she reached under her and got the egg.

"So that's the way you do it," Rob said.

"You want to try your hand at milking?" Emma asked. "I only milk Short Ears."

"Short Ears?"

"When she was a calf, the tips of her ears froze off one winter. We give all our cows names that fit them. There's Muley—Papa milks her because she has a mind of her own. And there's Old Lady, because her hide is sprinkled with white hairs."

"Well, it doesn't matter what their names are. I've never milked a cow. You'd have to show me."

Emma laughed. "Tonight I'll teach you how to milk," she said.

School that day went smoothly. She noticed that Rob didn't react when the others called him Smartypants, so they quit doing it.

When she finished doing her sums and was waiting for the teacher to give her something else to do, Emma made a list of cholera symptoms. She wrote it in the notebook she kept for her observations. If she and Rob wrote down everything they had learned from Dr. Drake's reading material, maybe it would help Rob's father. Uncle Anthony probably hadn't had the time to read all the medical magazines the way they had.

*Cholera Symptoms*

*1. diarrhea*
*2. vomiting*
*3. stomach cramps*
*4. blue skin*
*5. cold hands and feet*

Those were all the symptoms she could recall. She stuck the paper in the pocket of her skirt, and after school when they got back to the house, she asked Miss Clara if she could talk to her.

"I want to know more about the cholera," she said.

"Why?"

Emma could see the look in her eye that said she didn't want to talk about it. "I want to give a list of symptoms to Uncle Anthony. That way he'll know what to watch for."

Miss Clara heaved a deep sigh. "It's a nasty disease, and I can't think of where Ruthann got it except from that apple she ate."

"That's probably it," Emma said. "Dr. Drake told us the disease is carried by invisible poisonous insects, sort of like gnats, but we can't see them. You know how gnats buzz around overripe apples? Maybe the cholera insects fly around not quite ripe apples."

"Maybe so." Miss Clara stared into space for a long moment. At last, she sighed and said, "First Ruthann got diarrhea real bad. Then she got to vomiting. Her stomach hurt her so much. It was like she was poisoned."

"Did her skin turn blue?" Emma asked.

"Near the end it did. How do you know so much about this?"

"I've read Dr. Drake's medical magazines. Were her hands cold?"

"Near to freezing. She couldn't get them warm—her feet neither. I put hot bricks in bed with her, but they didn't help." A tear rolled down Miss Clara's lined face. "I couldn't do anything to help her."

Emma couldn't think what to say that would comfort Miss Clara. "Thank you." She gave Miss Clara's shoulder an awkward pat, wishing there was something more she could do. Miss Clara leaned her head against Emma's shoulder, and after a minute, Emma put her arms around the old lady. Miss Clara sobbed against her dress, and Emma found herself comforting her the way she would her little sister, Mary. Old ladies and little girls weren't so different, she realized. They both just needed to know that some-one still loved them, that they weren't all alone in the world.

"It's a filthy disease," Miss Clara said, raising her head at last. "Some say it's punishment coming from God's own hand, but why would He punish my Ruthann?"

"I don't think it's God's punishment," Emma said. That was the first time she'd said it out loud, but she had been thinking about it ever since the preacher had brought up the idea that the drunks down in Shantytown were getting sick because of their sin.

"If you get the disease, it's because the invisible insects got to you," Emma said, "not because God wants to strike you dead. He couldn't have picked out Miss Ruthann. The insects got her."

"Dr. Drake said since she was already feeling poorly, she was weak and an easy target for the cholera. I don't rightly understand it, Emma," Miss Clara said.

Emma nodded. She didn't rightly understand it either, no matter how she tried.

All afternoon, Emma looked for Rob, but he was nowhere to be found. "I think I saw him heading off into the woods," Sue Ellen said.

*Maybe he wants to be alone again,* Emma reasoned. By suppertime, he was back, and that evening, he tried his hand at milking. All he did was provide Emma with a good belly laugh that made her feel better after her serious discussion with Miss Clara. He tried different ways of pulling on the teats, but he couldn't get so much as a drop of milk out.

"You pull and squeeze at the same time," Emma said. "There's a rhythm to it." She sat down on the three-legged stool and showed him one more time. The warm milk made a *ping-ping* sound as it hit the side of the bucket.

Again, Rob took the place on the stool and tried it. He pulled. He squeezed. Short Ears bawled. Then she kicked her hind leg out, scaring Rob so much he tipped over the pail, spilling the milk that Emma already had gotten in the bucket.

"I guess I'll go back to collecting the eggs," Rob said, and Emma held her stomach because she laughed so hard.

On Sunday, Anthony arrived not long after sunup. After breakfast, the families rode in the wagon to the schoolhouse, where a traveling preacher talked about the wrath of God that had descended on Cincinnati and the curse on the immoral and ungodly.

Emma and Miss Clara exchanged a glance, and Emma shook her head. She stared belligerently at the preacher. She turned to voice her protest to her mother, but Mama patted her arm and whispered, "We'll talk later."

After Sunday dinner, the whole family walked down to the creek, and Rob showed his parents where he and Emma measured the height of the water.

"Dr. Drake sends a message," Anthony said as they stood by the creek. "He sees no evidence that the vicious and poverty-stricken and drunkards are more liable to get the disease than temperate people who never take a drink of alcohol. He didn't want anyone thinking that Miss Ruthann was taking a nip now and then."

"I didn't think that," Emma put in. "I think anyone that the insects attack is going to get it." She dug in her pocket for the list she had made. "Here are the symptoms. I made them for you so you would know what to look for."

Rob took the list from her and scowled at it, then handed it to his father. "At the first sign, you must run to Dr. Drake, Father. At the first sign!" Rob repeated. "I remember reading that half the people who get cholera will die. The other half, if they can be treated in time, will live. At the first sign, you must be treated!"

"How old are you?" his father asked with a smile.

"Eleven on Tuesday," Rob answered.

"I'm not so sure. Sometimes I think you're older than me," he said. "You sound like my father." He reached over and tousled Rob's blond hair, then turned to Emma. "Thank you, Emma, for writing this down for me. I'll keep it with me."

They walked back up to the house and sat in the yard on chairs and quilts, taking advantage of the late September sunshine until it was time for Anthony to return to Cincinnati. Patricia held his hand and clung to him as long as she could.

Emma overheard her ask, "How many have died?"

"Over a hundred and fifty this week," he said. "But don't worry about me. I'll be fine." He bent down and kissed Patricia. She stood and watched until he was out of sight.

Emma looked around for Rob, but he was nowhere to be seen. She figured he was out in the woods again, and she frowned. What if he had discovered her secret? With an hour still to go before sunset, she decided to take a walk out in the woods herself. Echo fluttered onto her shoulder, and she made her way through the pasture and then followed the path up into the woods. When she came to the branch of the creek that ran through the woods, she walked parallel to it until she came to the ford in the creek, where stepping rocks stuck out of the water. Tiptoeing carefully, she balanced on the rocks and made it across without even getting the toes of her shoes wet. On the other side of the creek, she saw deer tracks. But they were oddly spaced. Three made deeper imprints in the soft creek bank than the other one. Odd.

Cautiously, she made her way along the bank. This was obviously a drinking hole for the deer. If she walked softly enough, maybe she would see one.

But where was Rob? What could he find to do with himself down here alone? The creek had always been her special place to go when she needed to be by herself; it felt a little strange now to be sharing it with Rob—and yet she knew he needed someplace to go when his worries about his father were overwhelming him. But what could he be doing down here so often? Just sitting and thinking?

Then she heard his voice coming from a thicket of trees that grew close along the water. "Good boy. Now hold still, little fellow."

"Good boy," the crow on her shoulder mimicked.

"Hush," Emma whispered. She was filled with curiosity. Who was Rob talking to?

She crouched behind a clump of bramble bushes and gingerly pushed a prickly branch out of the way so she could see him.

"That's it," Rob was saying. "Let me get a good look. We might take this off today, little fellow."

He was bending over a young fawn, his arms encircling its head to hold it still. His hands reached down to touch its leg. Wooden splints were wrapped tightly with twine.

"Rob," Emma said in a soft voice so she wouldn't disturb the deer.

His head shot up, but he didn't let go of the deer. It struggled in his grasp, evidently alarmed by the sudden stiffness of his arms.

"Go away," he said in a low voice, one that said he meant it.

"I'll help you," Emma said and quickly let go of the bramble branch, which pricked her finger. She stuck it in her mouth and sucked on it for a second as she came out from behind the bush. "When did he break his leg?"

"Go away," Rob repeated, his voice still low so he wouldn't upset the deer.

"Has the splint been on long enough? I can hold him for you so you can take it off."

"I can take care of him," he said. "Good boy. Hold still." The deer stomped a hoof.

Emma advanced one slow step at a time. When she was beside Rob, she knelt down and calmly stroked the deer. "Are you going to let me help you or not?" she asked.

"All right." He sighed, giving in. "Grab his back feet, and we'll lay him down. Then I'll hold him tight while you cut this twine."

Emma saw a butcher knife lying on the ground nearby. "This could hurt him."

"I know, but it's time. Now! Turn him."

Rob was practically sitting on the animal, holding him down.

Emma knelt in front of the deer, petting him and crooning softly. She waited until the animal had settled down and then reached for the knife. With a swift, deft movement, she cut the knot. The fawn reared, but Rob held on tight and calmed him until Emma could unwind the twine and release the crude splints. She felt the leg and moved it gently back and forth.

"Feels strong. Let him up."

Rob jumped back, and the deer sprang to its feet. It favored the broken leg but darted back into the underbrush and away.

"Why didn't you tell me?" Emma asked.

"Why should I?" he asked. "You would have just taken over, the way you always do. You always think you know more than me, and I'm tired of it. I found him when I was down here missing Father. I thought it would be a good chance for me to practice being a doctor."

"But you should have told me," Emma insisted. "I could have helped you." She was filled with a sudden strange achy feeling that she had no name for. It felt a little like jealousy, but it felt even more like disappointment. She blinked away her tears. "You always talk about being a doctor, and everyone encourages you. Dr. Drake will help you, and your parents are proud of you. Everyone says how everyone can be what he wants to be in this great country." She glared at Rob as though everything was his fault. "Well, not everybody can. I want to be a doctor for animals. Do you think that's likely for a girl?"

CHAPTER 12

# Emma Shares Her Secret

After her outburst, Emma stormed off. She felt both guilty and hurt that Rob hadn't trusted her enough to tell her about the fawn. She *was* bossy sometimes, she acknowledged to herself. But sometimes she felt so frustrated, knowing that she had good ideas and that most people wouldn't listen to her just because she was a girl. At least with Rob, she always knew she could make him do what she wanted.

She walked deeper into the hills with Echo on her shoulder, glad to be by herself for a change. She liked having the Etingoffs and Miss Clara staying with them, but she also felt as though life was busier and more crowded than it usually was. People were everywhere you turned—and her head felt crowded, too, stuffed full of new worries, old resentments, and strange ideas to consider.

"Sometimes," she whispered to Echo, "I don't like being me." She considered praying about her feelings, but she didn't know how to shape the words. After all, God had made her a girl, so He must have wanted her to accept her lot in life.

"But maybe He doesn't," she told Echo, new thoughts struggling to take shape in her mind. "Maybe it's like the cholera insects. They don't come from God—and He expects us to do all we can to avoid them so people won't die." Emma sat down on a rock, thinking hard. "I know it's not right for me to be mean to Rob when I'm just frustrated he can do more things than I can because he's a boy." She was still talking out loud, but she was no longer certain if she was talking to Echo or to God. Maybe she was praying after all. "I don't want to just give in and accept that Rob can be anything he wants but I can't. Maybe that's not the way it's supposed to be. Maybe girls *should* be allowed to be anything they want, just like boys. Maybe. . .maybe You want me to work hard to change things, the same way we've all been working so hard to fight the cholera."

She felt strange saying all this to God, but she also felt a funny little prickle of something like hope. Mama always told her that all things work together for good for those who love God. Emma didn't like it when Mama told her that, because it seemed like just giving in and accepting all the bad things in life. But now, for the first time, Emma realized the Bible verse didn't mean that at all. She struggled to think through what the verse did mean. *Maybe,* she thought, groping for words, *it means that if we give ourselves to God and let Him use us, He'll take all the mixed-up things and all the sad things and all the wonderful things and pull them all together into something. . .well, something good. Something that will make us happy—and that will make Him happy, too.*

Her thoughts turned to her dreams for the future. Were there women who took care of animals? She'd never heard of one. Would she be strong enough? She'd been big enough to handle the fawn—but what about a cow or a horse? Of course, usually when a cow or a horse broke its leg, people just shot the animal and put it out of its misery. But that wouldn't be what Emma would do, not if she had her way. She had insisted they return the flood-trapped snakes to the Ohio River, and she would try to save any animal.

It was almost dark. Time for her to head back to the house. Her head was still full of mixed-up thoughts, and she still felt angry and guilty—but at the same time, she felt hopeful and a little excited.

She slipped through the back door into the kitchen. The sound of the adults' voices came to her from the parlor, and then Rob came into the kitchen. He must have heard the sound of the screen door slapping shut behind her.

"I need a drink of water." He didn't look at her as he walked over to the water bucket and lowered the dipper. As he drank the water, though, he turned to face her and met her eyes. He hung the dipper back on the rim of the bucket.

"No, I have never heard of a girl being an animal doctor." He answered her earlier question as if she'd just asked it instead of an hour having passed since they last spoke. He continued in the same low voice so the adults wouldn't hear. "But that doesn't mean you can't be the first. You were a big help to me with the deer. I bet you could have done it all by yourself."

She took her turn at the water bucket, then faced him. "How did you get the splint on him? Didn't he try to kick you?"

"I knocked him out with a rock."

"You hit the deer?"

"What else could I do? He was in bad pain. I figured if I killed him, it would be better than what he was going through, but if it just knocked him out, maybe I could fix him up. He was already down. Anyway, they shoot horses that break their legs, so I figured that if I killed him, that might be the right thing. I figured even if he died, I could work on the leg and learn about it. I ran up here and got the supplies I'd need, then I clunked him with a big rock. Once I saw that he was still breathing, I put the splint on. I didn't know if I got the bone in the right place, but it felt right. I stayed with him until he woke up, and I gave him water and some grain.

He trusted me, but when I left him that night, I didn't know if he'd be gone or worse—dead—when I went back the next day."

Emma leaned against the kitchen table beside Rob. It felt good to be talking with him instead of arguing with him. "I fixed a rabbit's broken foot once," she confided.

Rob looked at her thoughtfully. "That's why you wanted that book on bones from the library, isn't it?"

Emma nodded. "I wanted to see if I'd fixed the rabbit's broken foot right. It had been caught in a trap. It ran away, and I haven't seen it since."

Rob smiled at her. "Guess you and I have even more in common than we realized."

Emma nodded and returned his smile.

"You two need to be getting to bed," Mama called from the parlor.

"Yes, Mama, we're going."

"Emma, why can't you be an animal doctor?" Rob asked in a quick whisper. "You sure enough like animals. You fixed up Echo."

"He was easy. I just caught worms and fed him milk until he was strong enough to fly away. Trouble is, he didn't want to fly off. He just stayed around. I guess he likes me," she said with a tinge of pride in her voice.

"Let's ask Dr. Drake about it. He'll know how to go about becoming an animal doctor." His brow wrinkled as he considered her problem. "Have you asked your mother about it?"

"No. I can't think she'd want me to be something like that. She'd say it was man's work. They're already talking about me quitting school in another year or so. They say so long as I know how to read and write, there's no point in me taking up my time sitting in school."

Rob nodded. "We'll talk to Dr. Drake about it," he said again.

"Whenever we can get back to Cincinnati."

Emma didn't want to leave the kitchen and go to bed, but she knew their mothers would scold them if they didn't go soon. She lingered a moment longer, though, wondering what Miss Clara would think if Emma confided her dreams to her. Miss Clara had never married and had a family like Mama—but still, all she had done her whole life was take care of the home she shared with her sister. Now Miss Ruthann—she was a different story. If a thing were possible, she probably wanted to try it. For such a frail woman, she had a strong backbone.

But she was dead now. For a moment, Emma had forgotten. When she remembered, she felt a welling up from inside that made it hard to swallow.

"We'd better get to bed," Rob said in a low voice.

A new thought occurred to Emma. Rob hadn't trusted her enough to tell her about the deer—but she hadn't ever trusted him enough, either. She'd been keeping a big secret from him—but now she wanted to share it. "Yes," she agreed, "but tomorrow after school, I'll show you something I've been working on."

"What?" he asked.

"Tomorrow," she said and walked toward the stairs.

The next day it seemed the teacher would never let school out. The walk home felt longer than normal, too. When they could finally see Emma's house, Rob broke into a run, but he must have realized it wouldn't do any good for him to get home any faster than Emma. He slowed to a walk, looking over his shoulder at Emma, and she gave him a grin and went on poking along with Sue Ellen and Timothy.

"We're going to go measure the creek, Mama," Emma said when they walked in the door. She put the lunch pail in the kitchen and walked out the back door with Rob on her heels. Echo flew from the barn roof and landed on her shoulder.

They hurried to the creek and really did measure the water, which was up a little bit from rain in the night.

"This can't be the surprise," Rob said. "I've known about your measuring notch on the tree trunk since the first day I came."

"Follow me," she said. They went farther upstream to the rocks, crossed the creek, then continued along the bank past the place where she had found Rob with the deer.

"Here," she said with a sweep of her hand.

"Here. Here," the crow on her shoulder mimicked.

Rob looked around. Emma held her breath, waiting for his reaction as he looked at the crates and coops of various sizes, all rather crudely built and extending to the edge of the water.

"This is my hospital," she said. "An animal hospital. Over here I have. . .well, come and see."

She led him to the first coop. It held several curled up young foxes.

"They're orphans," she said. "The mother was probably shot for raiding henhouses. Anyway, when I found them, I didn't touch them for two days, waiting for her to come back. She never came."

"What do you feed foxes?"

"That's a problem. I don't have any dead chickens, so I've been giving them eggs." She giggled. "Remember all those eggs you broke the first day you helped with the chores? Well, I made sure they went to good use." She knelt down next to the cages. "I have their pen partly in the water so they can get a drink whenever they want." It felt good to finally share her secret with someone.

113

Rob reached in to pet one of the foxes, but Emma stopped him.

"Oh, you can't treat them like kittens, even though they might look like them. They're wild, and they have to be able to return to the wild when they're big enough."

Rob jerked back. "When will that be?"

"Another couple weeks. Over here," she said and waved her hand, "is a rabbit. It was also caught in a trap, but it didn't die. I don't know who's setting traps on our land. I get rid of them when I find them."

"Why don't these animals bite you when you put a splint on them?"

Emma looked half ashamed, half defiant. "I put a bag over their head and tie it tight. After a while, they don't struggle so much. It's the only way I know how to help them."

"And you sounded upset with me for clunking the deer over the head!" Rob grinned. "Have you killed any?"

"A possum never did wake up."

"You sure it wasn't fooling you?" Rob said with a laugh. "Playing possum on you?"

"He was dead. There was no heartbeat. I made sure before I cut him open."

Rob's mouth flew open, and he left the rabbit crate and faced Emma.

"You cut him open?"

"Like Dr. Drake said about the skeleton in his office. That's how you learn about the parts. You were going to do the same thing with the deer," she reminded him.

Rob looked around. "Where's the skeleton?"

"Over here." She lifted a solid crate that was high on the bank, not near the water. "I had to boil him to get the meat off, like you would a pig's head to make head cheese. I was careful not to disturb any of the bones, but they came apart because there weren't any muscles left. It was like boiling a chicken. I should have known that."

Rob looked at the skeleton with great interest. Emma had tied the bones together with twine, and in places she'd used nails. It didn't look exactly like a possum, but she'd done a pretty good job.

"Do you think animal doctors ever operate on animals? I mean, they're not like people."

"Oh, I know, but I thought it would help to see the bones."

"Probably animal doctors give animal medicine to the sick ones."

"Or the same medicine. I heard Papa say that the cholera doctors in Cincinnati are giving calomel to children in amounts that are fit for a horse."

Rob caught his breath as though he'd run into something nasty. Emma knew what he was thinking. "I'm sorry," she said softly. "I didn't mean to remind you of the cholera. I know you're worried about your father and all your friends in town."

"I'm fine," Rob muttered and lifted his head. "So, you have the foxes and a rabbit. That's all?"

"That's all right now," she said. "I could have more tomorrow. It depends on what I find that's hurt."

The next day on the road to school, they found a hawk that was riddled with buckshot.

"Somebody missed a clean shot, I suspect," Emma said. "It could only fly this far before falling."

They didn't have to knock the bird out, because it was already lying down, barely breathing. It didn't put up a fight when Emma picked it up.

"What can you do for it?" Rob asked.

"I don't know, but I'll take it home after school and give it some water."

She placed it under a tree near the schoolyard, and when noon arrived, she and Rob went out to look at the bird. It was already dead.

"Will you cut it up?" Rob asked.

Emma shook her head and didn't answer for a moment. "It's too much like a chicken, and I know what they look like inside."

It didn't seem right to leave it there under the tree. Rob found a stout stick and dug a hole in the ground where it was fairly soft. Emma placed the bird in the shallow grave, and together they covered it with dirt. There weren't any flowers around to decorate the grave, but the sumac leaves had already turned brilliant red, so they picked a few stems and planted them in the dirt.

"Should we say some words over him?" Rob asked.

"Ashes to ashes, dust to dust." Emma used the same words her father had said in their memorial service for Miss Ruthann. "Do you think animals go to heaven?"

"I don't know," Rob said. "I don't know about that."

That night, they had birthday cake with supper, and the others called out "Happy birthday!" to Rob.

"Your father is sorry he couldn't be here, but he sends his love and this," Patricia said. She handed him a book. "It's one that Dr. Drake recommended. Happy birthday."

Rob leafed through the medical dictionary. "It's perfect," he said. "Thank you, Mother."

Later that evening before they went to bed, he read the inscription in the front out loud to Emma. "To my son, who will someday be a great doctor because he cares about people. With love, Father."

"You're lucky," Emma said softly. "Your father understands about your dreams."

The next morning, Papa headed to town for market day, but he returned early that afternoon just as Emma and the others got home from school. He wore a solemn expression, and he pulled the rig up in front of the house instead of driving it to the barn.

"Emma," he called, and she and Rob ran up to him. "Put the team up for me."

"Papa, what's wrong?" she asked.

"I need to talk to your mother," he said and climbed down from the wagon, handing her the reins.

Rob climbed on board with Emma, and she drove the team to the barn and parked the wagon. He helped her unhitch the horses, and while the animals drank greedily from the water trough, he and Emma brushed them down.

Emma kept glancing toward the house. "Something's wrong," she said. "Something's really wrong." Her heart felt as though it were stuck in her throat as she thought of Rob's father in Cincinnati with the cholera insects. But if Uncle Anthony was sick, wouldn't Papa have said he needed to talk to Aunt Patricia?

As soon as they put the horses in their stalls, Rob and Emma ran for the house. They burst into the kitchen, but no one was there. They found everyone in the parlor, sitting in stunned silence. Papa hugged Mama, who looked pale and had tears streaming down her cheeks.

"Who died?" Rob asked in a tight voice.

"One of the cousins," Uncle Thomas answered. "Amos Riley. The funeral was this morning. His brother Sam came to the market to get me. Amos had sent the rest of his family away. They don't know he's dead yet."

Mama sobbed, and Papa held her head against his chest. Emma thought about Amos, a man who was a little younger than Mama. The last time they'd seen him had been at the Fourth of July picnic. They weren't as close to the Rileys as they were to the Etingoffs, but it seemed impossible to think that Amos was dead. She had known him ever since she was born.

She looked at Rob and saw that he was fighting back tears. She knew he was upset about Amos, but he was also scared about his father. Emma tried to think what she could do to make everything not seem so awful. An idea occurred to her.

She walked into the bedroom and returned with her mother's harmonica. Emma handed the harmonica to her mother. "I think Amos would want you to play a hymn for him. And it might make us feel better, too."

CHAPTER 13

# Rob's Worst Fear

"Please don't go back on market day," Mama said to Papa at the supper table that night. "You might never return."

"Could we talk about this later?" he asked and gave a slight nod toward Rob and the others.

"Yes, I'm sorry," Mama said quickly. "More potatoes, Miss Clara?" she said in a falsely bright voice.

Emma stole a look at Rob and his mother, who sat rigidly, not saying anything. Patricia had been very quiet after the service they'd held for Amos. She wasn't crying. She just stared into space as if she weren't seeing anything.

Emma felt as if she could barely breathe. First Miss Ruthann had died, and now Amos. Papa had explained how Miss Ruthann was old and frail and easily succumbed to the cholera. But Amos? He had been a strong man. Strong like Uncle Anthony.

The families were quiet that October night, and they all went to bed earlier than usual. But Emma lay awake long after.

Morning started in the same way as always. Rob collected eggs, and Emma milked the cows with Papa. The children went to school. But Emma knew nothing would be the same for Rob until Sunday morning when his father rode into the yard. Her heart ached for her cousin.

When Sunday finally came, the first light brought with it the sound of hooves coming up the lane. Emma and Rob were sitting on the front porch waiting, and she felt Rob release a pent-up breath he must have been holding for a long time. It was as if his whole body had been bound up like that deer's leg in the splint. Now the twine that bound it had been cut, and he was free again. As Anthony's horse rounded the curve in the lane, Emma smiled and breathed a prayer of thanksgiving.

"Father's home!" Rob shouted.

His mother rushed outside as his father pulled up the horse by the porch. Before he had even completely dismounted, Patricia had wrapped her arms around him. They held each other tight and then pulled Rob and Sue Ellen into their embrace.

"I'm so glad you're here," Patricia said. "Come tell us the news."

"Good morning," Anthony said to the others who were gathered in the parlor. "Thomas, I knew Kristen had tied you up when you didn't come to town yesterday."

"Just about," Papa said with a slow grin. "She's got a pretty good grip on me."

"It's just as well. Half the people have left town."

"Then can you stay, too?" Rob's mother asked.

He looked at her and shook his head no. "We have an order for this steamboat we're working on, and we need to finish it. I gave my word."

"But your life is more important. . . ." Patricia stopped herself and gave that tight smile Emma was getting used to.

There was no preacher at church at the little schoolhouse that Sunday. He was preaching at another tiny congregation on the other side of Cincinnati where folks were also afraid to drive into town for a church service. Instead of hearing preaching, the folks sang hymns and then they held a prayer circle. Young and old held hands, and each person said a prayer as his or her turn came.

"Thank You for this good day," Patricia said, "and please keep my husband safe."

"Thank You for this day, and please let Father not catch the cholera," Sue Ellen said next.

"Thank You for this day and for Your Son, and please stop the cholera from killing any more people," Mama said.

And it was the same as the prayer made the circle. The cholera was at the front of everyone's mind.

Over Sunday dinner, the family asked Anthony for news of the various people they knew in town. Mostly, he had good news to tell. Many folks had left town to escape the disease that lurked within the city limits.

"What about Dr. Drake?" Rob asked.

"He's all right. Just worn out from trying to take care of so many people."

Patricia clutched his hand. "I wish you didn't have to go back there."

"I won't get sick," Anthony said.

"I know you won't," she said, "but be careful."

"I promise. But don't you worry." He kissed her on the forehead and hugged her tight.

"How many?" Patricia asked. "How many have died?"

Anthony hesitated. "Dr. Drake says around four hundred."

"In just two weeks!" Mama exclaimed.

"Father, do you have Emma's list?" Rob asked, referring to the list of cholera symptoms.

His father smiled at the children and patted his pocket. "I have it right here."

"At the first sign—"

"I know," his father interrupted him. Emma could tell he didn't want to talk any more about the cholera. "I'll see you next Sunday." He kissed Patricia again and climbed on his horse.

The days fell into a pattern. Up early to do chores, to school, to the creek to measure the water and check on the animals, to bed, up early to do chores. Midweek market day came and went, and Papa stayed on the farm, much to Mama's relief.

"It's a good day to dig sprouts out of the pasture," he told Rob and Emma. "Can't have our best milkers tripping over sprouts."

As he turned away, Rob nudged Emma. "Whoever heard of cows tripping on tree sprouts?" he asked. "He's just making an excuse for not going to market."

"He doesn't want to go where the cholera is," Emma agreed soberly. "That's just common sense. He could die if he went into town." She didn't want Rob thinking that her father was a coward, but then she wanted to bite her tongue; she hadn't meant to remind him that his own father was in danger.

By Thursday, she could tell Rob was so worried about his father that he was having a hard time getting from one minute to the next. "Miss Ruthann, dead. Amos, dead." He muttered the list in a low voice as they walked home from school one afternoon. "Who will be next, do you suppose?" His voice was filled with dread, and Emma longed to say something that would comfort him. . .but she couldn't think of anything.

On Friday morning, Emma and Rob gathered the eggs and

walked with the others to school. "Two more days," he said.

"Until when?" Emma asked absently. She was thinking about the animals in her hospital, and she wasn't really paying attention.

"Until Sunday." Rob sounded surprised Emma didn't know what he was talking about. "Until Father comes. Until I know he's safe. Sometimes I don't see how I can live through another day not knowing."

Emma again searched for words that might make him feel better. "At least school is better now. Mr. LaRose doesn't seem quite so strict. And everyone calls you *Rob* now instead of *Smartypants.*" She smiled, but no answering smile crossed Rob's face.

"It doesn't matter," he said in a flat voice. "Nothing matters, so long as Father is safe."

After school, the two of them walked aimlessly down to the creek, more out of habit than out of any desire to measure the height of the water. Emma told him she had seen the deer yesterday and that it was running just as if it had never broken its leg. She had thought he would be interested, but instead he barely seemed to hear her. So she talked about the rabbit. She talked and she talked, but he just stared into space.

"Come on, slowpoke," she called as she ran ahead of him to the partly submerged notched tree. She recorded the depth of the water.

"Slowpoke. Slowpoke," her pesky crow said.

"Leave me alone," Rob answered, his voice sharp. He glared at Echo. "I'm tired of that crow. And I'm tired of measuring the water. It didn't make any difference. It didn't make the cholera go away. It didn't prove anything."

"But we don't know yet," Emma protested. "If we're going to be scientists, we need to keep track of all sorts of information. You never know what will prove useful."

Rob just shrugged and kicked a stone.

They walked in silence for a moment, and then Emma said, "I wonder if we should let the foxes go today. They're getting bigger, and I want them to—"

"Be quiet!" Rob yelled at her. "I don't care about your animals. They're just dumb animals. They don't matter."

All Emma's good resolutions about being nice to Rob suddenly disappeared. "What's wrong with you? They are not dumb animals!" she shouted back at him.

"Yes, they are. They are!" Rob was screaming now, right into her face. "They don't matter. They're not people. They're not dying." Tears flooded his eyes, and he brushed them away furiously. "They don't matter!" he yelled again as the tears ran down his cheeks.

"Crybaby!" Emma shouted.

"Crybaby. Crybaby," Echo said in his bird voice.

Rob picked up a stone and jerked his hand back as though he was going to throw it at Echo. Before he could, Emma turned around and sped away from him. "I hate you, Rob Etingoff!" she shouted over her shoulder.

She heard him sob behind her, but she was too furious with him to care. She kept running until she reached the house. Echo flew away with a squawk as Emma banged through the screen door.

Inside the kitchen, Mama was paring potatoes. For once, she was alone, without Patricia or Miss Clara or even Mary, and Emma leaned her hot, angry face against her mother's soft shoulder.

Mama wiped her hands and then held Emma away from her while her eyes searched Emma's face. "What is it?" she asked.

"It's Rob," Emma choked. "He makes me so angry. He wanted to throw a rock at Echo just now."

"That doesn't sound like Rob. He must have been pretty upset."

Emma nodded. "He said animals were just dumb, that they didn't matter. He told me to be quiet when I was just trying to cheer him up."

Mama smoothed Emma's hair away from her forehead. "And what did you say to him?"

Emma bit her lip. "I called him a crybaby," she muttered finally, filled with guilt.

"Sounds like you owe him an apology."

"He owes me one, too," Emma said stubbornly.

Mama picked up the knife and began paring the potatoes again. "He's scared, Emma. He and Patricia are both so worried about Anthony that they can barely think. We need to do everything we can to help them. This is a terrible time for them."

"But I don't know what to do to help him."

Mama smiled as she dropped a potato into a pot of water. "You could start by praying for him. And if you have a chance, maybe you could encourage him to give his fear to God. God is our only hope in times like these."

Emma picked up a potato and another knife and began to help her mother. "Do you think God will protect Anthony from the cholera?" she asked softly.

"I don't know," Mama said. "But I do know that whatever happens, God can use it for good, so long as we commit our ways to Him."

"That's what you always say."

Mama laughed. "That's because it's true."

Rob didn't come back for supper. After the dishes were done, Mama gave Emma a little push toward the back door. "Go find him," she whispered. "He's been alone long enough now."

Emma made her way up the hill to the trees. "Rob," she called. "Rob!"

"I'm here," came a small, flat voice from the shadows beneath a tree.

Emma crouched down beside him on the dried leaves. "I'm sorry," she said.

He turned his head and looked at her, as though he were surprised. "Why? I'm the one who was mean to you about your animals."

Emma nodded. "But I called you a crybaby. I'd be scared, too, if it were my father who was in town with the cholera. I'd be crying all the time." She touched his arm. "I'm truly sorry, Rob. Mama says we should pray. She says that no matter what happens, God will work things out."

"But I don't want anything to happen to my father. If anything happened to him, I don't see how God could work that out."

"I know." Emma shifted herself so she could sit cross-legged beside him. "I guess maybe that's when we need to pray the most—when we're scared and it's hard to have faith."

Rob was silent for a long moment. "All right," he said finally. "Will you pray out loud for me?"

Emma hesitated. She never really liked praying so people could hear her, but Rob needed her. He and she had been through a lot. They'd captured snakes together in the flooded house. They'd learned about medical things. She'd confided about her dream of being an animal doctor, and he'd told her about wanting to be a doctor. He didn't like the country that much, but she wasn't crazy about the town, either. They were different, and they were the same. She could trust him not to laugh at her.

"Dear God," she said softly, "be with Rob's father. Take care of him. Please keep him safe. And be with Rob and his mother. Help Rob not to feel so scared. Help him to know You're with him. . . and You're with his father, too. Help us to trust You, even when we're scared. Amen."

"Amen," Rob whispered. He raised his head. "Thanks, Emma."

Emma smiled at him. "Let's go back home. We've already eaten supper, but Mama saved you some beans and cornbread."

When they walked in the kitchen door, Rob's mother held out her arms to him. She held him tight and kissed the top of his head.

"You should be a carefree boy," she said. "But you're a young man already." She stepped back. "You must be hungry."

She pulled out a chair from the table, and Rob sat down to eat a bowl of beans.

Saturday dawned clear and bright but with an October chill in the air.

"I'm sorry about calling your animals dumb," Rob said as he and Emma walked down to the creek.

"That's okay. They aren't important like people dying, but that doesn't mean I want to help them any less."

Emma recorded the creek depth, while Rob looked up at the bright blue sky.

"No clouds. Emma, how can cholera be spread by bad atmosphere when it's such a clear, sunny day?"

She stared at the sky. "Maybe it's not so clear in Cincinnati."

"It's only a few miles away. We should be able to see a few miles in the sky, shouldn't we? I wish we could go to the library and find that book about clouds. I wish we could ask Dr. Drake what he thinks about this."

Emma tried to turn his thoughts in a different direction. "Let's check on the animals. I think it's time to turn the foxes loose."

Together they lifted the coop off the curled-up foxes. They didn't move.

"We'd better leave so they can go," Rob said.

Emma wanted to watch, so they ran to the crossing rocks and then made their way stealthily upstream on the opposite side of the animal hospital.

"Look there," Emma whispered. The foxes had scampered to the water's edge and were drinking. Then one darted toward the brush, and another one followed, and then the third one.

"Think they'll make it?" Rob asked.

Emma nodded with pride. "They have a better chance than if they'd been left alone. Let's go."

As twilight fell that evening, the family heard hoofbeats on the road. The beats slowed as the rider turned up the lane to the house.

Rob's mother was the first one outside, but Rob was close behind her.

"Anthony?" Emma heard Patricia call into the growing darkness.

"Mrs. Etingoff, it's me, Andrew Hollister," the rider called out.

"Andrew? What's wrong with Anthony?" Panic laced her voice until it was a shrill shriek.

The man from Anthony's shipyard dismounted and tied his horse to a post on the porch. "Can we go inside?" he asked.

Patricia walked into the parlor as if she were in a trance. Rob and Andrew Hollister followed. Everyone was standing: Miss Clara by the fire, Mama and Papa who had been sitting on the settee, even the younger children who had been playing on the floor. They all watched in silence as Andrew Hollister crossed over to the fireplace and extended his hands to the warmth.

"I have a message from Anthony. He's ill. He said he has the first sign."

## CHAPTER 14

# A Ride to Cincinnati

Patricia put her hand over her heart and sat down hard in a chair.

"He also said for you to stay in the country," Andrew said. "He has kept his promise; now you are to promise you will stay in the country."

"No," Patricia said. "I made no such promise to him."

"I could sure use a cup of coffee before I go back," Andrew said. "In the kitchen?" He looked pointedly at Rob and Sue Ellen.

"Yes, coffee in the kitchen," Patricia said dully, as though she hardly knew what she was saying.

"Of course," Mama agreed. "In the kitchen."

The adults hurried from the parlor.

"They don't want us to hear what they're talking about," Emma whispered to Rob. "As if we're too young to know."

"I'm going to town," Rob whispered. "I've got to go. Now. Remember what Dr. Drake said: Cholera could take a life in six hours. I'm going to Father."

"We'll ride one of Papa's horses."

"You're going, too?" he whispered.

"I know my way in the dark. You don't." In a loud voice, she said, "We're going to check on the horse."

She slipped on her shawl, and Rob grabbed his coat. They went out the front door and circled around to the barn. The full moon lit the way.

Emma slipped the bridle on the mare and led her out of her stall. "Carry that saddle outside." She pointed to one that straddled a wooden railing.

Together they saddled the horse in the moonlight. Emma climbed in the saddle, and Rob sat in front of her. She guided the horse through the pasture. "We don't want them to know we're gone yet," she said. "The grass will muffle the mare's steps."

They had gone maybe half a mile before Emma turned the horse toward the road. "Hold on. We're going for a ride," Emma said. She made a clicking sound with her tongue, and the horse took off. She slowed the horse to a walk a couple times, just for a rest, then urged her on again. They were in Cincinnati in under a half hour.

The city was quiet. A hush seemed to have settled over it since the last time Emma had been there, almost three weeks ago now. No wagons rolled down the streets, and many homes were in darkness. A few had soft lantern light pouring from a window.

Emma wrinkled her nose at the smell of burning tar. She remembered that some people thought burning tar would keep away the cholera, but she wondered if it did anything but make the air stink.

The horse's hooves made a clomping sound on the pavement that echoed in the ghostly city. As she pulled on the reins, she couldn't help feeling as though they had ridden into a city of the dead.

"Why are we going slower?" Rob asked. "We have to hurry."

Emma clicked her tongue again. "Where are we going?"

"I don't know. Father could be at the hospital or at the pest-house or at home." He hesitated. "We're close to the hospital. Let's go there first. Remember, Father said he would consult Dr. Drake at the first sign."

"Dr. Drake will probably be at the hospital," Emma agreed.

Rob slid off the horse once they stopped in front of the hospital and ran inside while Emma tied up the horse and wiped it down. Then she hurried to catch up with Rob.

"Sister," he was saying to a nun who was scurrying down a narrow hall carrying a bucket, "I'm looking for my father, Anthony Etingoff. Is he here?"

"Anthony Etingoff," she repeated in a tired voice. "Yes, he was here, but now he's gone."

Rob leaned on the wall as though his legs suddenly had no strength. *No,* thought Emma. *Please don't let us be too late.*

"Dr. Drake took him home," the sister continued. "We have no empty beds."

"He's alive?" Rob asked in a shaky voice.

"Oh, what have I done?" The black-robed woman reached out to Rob. "I meant he was gone from the hospital, not gone from this earth. He's at his home."

Rob was already running toward the door. "Thank you," Emma called over her shoulder as she followed him.

It seemed like a lifetime, but only a few minutes passed before they were on Rob's street. A horse and buggy were tied up in front of the house, and a light glowed from the parlor window.

Rob jumped from the horse and raced to the house. He threw open the front door. No one was in the front room, but a lantern sat on a parlor table. "Father?" he said in a low voice. He walked hesitantly toward the bedroom. Emma followed him, afraid of what they might find.

"Rob? Is that you?" Emma recognized Dr. Drake's voice before the doctor stepped out of the bedroom.

"How's Father?"

"He's got cholera, but I think he's getting treatment in time. I'm just taking leeches off him now. Then I've got to get back to the hospital. You can take over here." He turned and walked back into the bedroom. Emma and Rob followed him.

Anthony lay in the bed, a pale figure against the white bedding. He wasn't blue. *That's a good sign,* Emma thought.

"Father!" Rob rushed to his side and leaned over and hugged him.

"Rob. My message was that you were not to come to town," his father said in a weak voice. "Where's your mother?"

"She's at Emma's. She doesn't know we came."

"Who's with you?"

"Emma. We'll take care of you."

"Good," Dr. Drake said. "Come in the parlor, and I'll give you instructions."

"I'll be right back, Father." Emma and Rob followed the doctor into the other room.

Dr. Drake seemed to notice Emma for the first time. "Good evening, Emma," he said. "I'm glad you've come, because I need to go, and I hated to leave Rob's father unattended. I'm giving him massive doses of laudanum so he's sedated while the calomel works." As he spoke, he wrote down instructions on paper he pulled from his pocket. "He may vomit again, but I hope we've stopped that. Rub his skin continually with this powered chalk. I'm all out of mercury ointment," he added, almost to himself.

"We can do that," Rob said confidently.

"Here are the leeches for bleeding him again. It's all on this paper. Follow the instructions, and I'll check on him again tomorrow." He turned to leave, then turned back. "You'll do just fine," he said.

"Well, let's get to work," Rob said once the doctor had gone. "I'll start the rubbing."

"I'll unsaddle the horse. I waited," she said uncertainly. "I didn't know what we'd find."

She didn't want to admit that she'd thought they might be making the dark journey back to the farm to tell Patricia and the others bad news.

"I know." Rob was smiling. "Thank God he's doing all right."

"Yes." Emma looked with wonder at Rob's face. "Rob, you were more scared yesterday than you are today when your father has cholera."

Rob thought about that for a moment. "You're right. I guess I stopped feeling so scared after you prayed. That's odd."

She smiled. "Maybe not so odd."

When Emma had taken care of the horse, she joined Rob in the sickroom, helping him give his father water and rubbing his skin with the chalk substance to keep him warm. They were determined not to let Anthony's skin turn blue. The laudanum was working its wonders, sedating Anthony so he didn't feel the intense stomach cramps Emma knew were one of the symptoms.

"What else should we do?" Emma asked at last when they had done everything the doctor had told them.

"Help me get the medicines lined up and write down the times for giving them." He handed her the instructions Dr. Drake had written. "Then you can sleep for a while. We'll trade off sleeping and rubbing Father's skin."

They got everything lined out, and Emma went to the other room to sleep. She fell asleep instantly, exhausted from everything that happened, but the sound of horses and a wagon outside roused her, and she stumbled out into the hallway. A moment later, Papa and Patricia burst into the house.

"Anthony," Patricia said and knelt beside the bed. She took

Anthony's hand and raised it to her lips.

"I told you not to come," he murmured.

"I had to come get your disobedient son." She gave Rob one of those looks that said she would deal with him later. "We're taking you to the country. I spoke with Dr. Drake at the hospital, and he says we can move you. As soon as he sees you in the morning, we'll go."

They took turns with Rob's father in the night, giving him medicine, placing the leeches on him, taking them off, and rubbing his skin. By morning he seemed better.

Dr. Drake returned a few hours later. He gave Anthony more medicine and told the children and Patricia that they were doing a splendid job. "I wish all my patients had this many nurses."

Emma and Rob walked with the doctor out to his rig.

"We've kept a log of the temperatures and the clouds and the wind," Rob said. "I don't see how any of them caused the cholera to breed. Should I keep writing them down?"

"Hmm. Sometimes, Rob, we prove something by disproving what we thought we could prove. Keep recording your data. When life gets back to normal, we'll look for patterns or abnormalities. You're going to make a fine doctor. I wish you were one now. I could use the help." He climbed up in his buggy. "Take care of your father. His recovery may be slow, but I think he'll make it."

"Thank you," Rob called after him.

There was much to be done. Papa had gone to Andrew Hollister's to discuss running the shipyard in Anthony's absence. Emma and Rob made a bed of heavy quilts in the back of the wagon. When Papa returned, the children heated bricks in the fireplace and put them in the bed to keep it warm while Patricia helped Anthony put on clean clothes.

When everything was ready, they all carried him to the bed in the wagon and covered him with more heavy quilts. Patricia climbed on board and drove the team while Emma and Rob sat in the back with Rob's father. They left Papa building a fire to burn the bed linen and clothes Anthony had worn when he got sick. Once the fire had burned out, Papa would ride the mare back to the farm.

As they rode out of town, Rob rubbed his father's face, the only part of his skin visible, since he was cocooned in quilts. As Emma watched him, in the distance, she heard church bells.

She had forgotten it was Sunday. There would be no time for church today. . .but Emma knew they were all worshiping in their hearts just the same.

## CHAPTER 15

# Safe at Last

The trip back to the farm took much longer than the trip in the darkness the night before. Rob worried about his father being cold, but his mother said he should be okay. He was probably sweating under all the heavy quilts. Anthony didn't say much, but he mumbled a couple times that he was all right. His eyes remained shut the entire trip.

Papa caught up with them before they were halfway home. "I'll ride ahead and have Kristen fix a place for Anthony," he said.

"We should isolate him," Rob's mother said.

"It's not contagious," Rob said. "He'll be all right with us."

"Just the same, we'll isolate him." His mother's voice was firm.

By the time Patricia turned the wagon into the Farleys' lane, Emma could see that Mama must have settled on the smokehouse as a quarantine place for Anthony. She and Miss Clara were out there with pails in their hands.

Sue Ellen ran toward the wagon. "We've carried all the meat to another shed," she said. "Uncle Thomas has started a fire, and we're moving a bed." She climbed up in the wagon and leaned over her father and kissed him. "I love you, Father." A tear rolled down her round cheek.

"He's going to be all right." Rob patted his sister on the back. He glanced at Emma, and she knew he hadn't realized that Sue

Ellen was scared, too, anymore than she had.

"The room's not quite ready," Mama said. "Are you okay in the wagon for a while, Anthony?" She had climbed up on a wheel and peered down at Anthony, since there was no more room in the wagon bed.

"The sunshine feels good on my face," Rob's father said. "I'm all right."

"Rob, heat up the bricks," his mother said.

He rummaged around until he located the bricks under the covers, disturbing his father as little as he could. Emma helped carry them to the fireplace and back to the wagon when they were hot.

"I could stay out here," Anthony said. "This feels good."

"It won't feel good tonight when there's a frost," his wife reminded him.

By the time they moved Rob's father into the smokehouse, it had been transformed into a bedroom. Emma recognized a table from the parlor, as well as the bed Patricia and Sue Ellen had been sleeping in. Two chairs from the front room were in there, too, and the place still had a smell from the lye soap Mama had used to clean it with. A fire burned brightly in the crude fireplace that was used to smoke meat.

Mama fixed a schedule so that someone was nursing Anthony at every minute, night and day. Soon everything had calmed down, and Miss Clara was taking her turn with Rob's father.

"I'm going down to the creek," Emma said, her hand on the kitchen doorknob that afternoon when they had finished eating the noon meal. "You coming, Rob?" She gave him a pointed stare, and he got up from his chair to fetch his coat.

"I sent Timothy down this morning to look after your animals," Mama said, "if that's why you're in such a hurry."

Emma gasped. "You know about my animals?"

Papa chuckled. "Do you think something can happen on my land that I wouldn't know about?"

"We were hoping you'd tell us what you were doing," Mama said.

"I didn't think you'd understand," Emma said.

"Understand what?" Mama moved around the kitchen table and put her hand on Emma's shoulder.

"That I like taking care of animals. I want to be an animal doctor." Emma looked down at the floor. "Ever heard of a girl wanting to do that?"

"I'll admit it's not common," Mama said. "But it's also uncommon for a girl to play a harmonica, and I wanted to do that, so I did. If you want to do something bad enough, you can find a way."

Emma hugged her mother. "I will find a way."

"Good," Papa said. "I could use some help with the farm animals. Maybe you ought to start studying about cattle and horses and pigs instead of foxes that raid our chicken coop."

Emma laughed out loud, her heart filled with both joy and relief.

"Maybe you should talk to Slim Watkins," Papa said. "Folks call on him when they need help with sick animals."

Emma's smile was a mile wide. "I'll do that."

Rob shrugged into his coat and joined Emma at the door.

"Can you imagine?" Emma said once they were outside. "They want me to be an animal doctor."

"Since you like the country so much, taking care of farm animals seems like the thing you ought to do," Rob said.

"And since you like the city so much, taking care of sick people at a hospital is what you should do," Emma said.

The two cousins grinned at each other.

They ran down to the creek and measured the water, and Rob jotted down their other observations. The injured rabbit was munching on some hay that Timothy had given it.

When they returned to the house, Patricia was taking her turn with Anthony, and Miss Clara sat at the kitchen table.

"How's Father?" Rob asked. His turn to nurse him was next.

"He's going to be fine," Miss Clara said. "He doesn't look at all like Ruthann did. He's getting pink color in his face. He's going to be fine."

Emma said a silent thank you to God. She'd been doing that on and off all day, but she couldn't say it enough to express the relief she felt.

Miss Clara's prediction was right. A week later, Rob's father insisted he be allowed up and around. Each day he grew stronger, and within a month he proclaimed himself to be better than before his bout with cholera.

Papa started going back into Cincinnati on market days. As winter moved in, the cholera lessened its hold on the town. Six weeks later, in mid-December, Miss Clara, Rob, Sue Ellen, and their mother and father packed their belongings on the wagon.

"Kristen, Thomas, I can't thank you enough for letting my family rely on you," Anthony said.

"Oh, Anthony, you'd have done the same for us," Mama said.

Rob stood to the side with Emma. "I'll miss the creek and the animals."

"Then come back sometime," she said. "Once I start going to school again, I'll see you every day. But for now, I'll be in town on Saturday, market day. We'll go talk to Dr. Drake."

"See you then." Rob climbed up on the wagon bed.

His father hollered "Giddap!" to the horses, and the family headed back to Cincinnati and their home.

With a sigh, Emma turned to go inside. She was going to miss spending so much time with Rob. . .but God had worked all things together for good, just as Mama had said He would.

Emma thought about her dreams for the future. She was glad to know that Mama and Papa supported her, but she still didn't know if she would ever get to be an animal doctor. *I guess I'll just have to wait to see how God works things out.*

If you enjoyed

# Emma's
## Secret

be sure to read other

# SISTERS IN TIME

books from BARBOUR PUBLISHING

- Perfect for Girls Ages Eight to Twelve

- History and Faith in Intriguing Stories

- Lead Character Overcomes Personal Challenge

- Covers Seventeenth to Twentieth Centuries

- Collectible Series of Titles

6" x 8 ¼" / Paperback / 144 pages / $3.97

AVAILABLE WHEREVER CHRISTIAN BOOKS ARE SOLD